Delaney's teeth clamped down on her lower lip and Jack nearly growled. He'd worry about exposing his past later. Right now he had better things to do.

Delaney's luscious mouth opened, forming a small *o*. Jack followed every nuance of her expression—from her initial hesitation to her eventual capitulation. He didn't realize he'd been holding his breath until his lungs started to burn.

He wanted this moment to be special for them both. Wanted her to want him as much as he desired her.

"What's stopping you?" she asked, challenge glinting in her mocha-colored eyes.

Her mouth widened into a smile that dared Jack to act.

Never one to back away from a challenge, he decided to begin with her mouth and work his way down from there....

Blaze

Dear Reader,

This is my first release for the Harlequin Blaze line. I'm so excited. I loved writing *Off Limits* because it gave me the chance to explore a setting that I'm very familiar with.

I was a flight attendant for fourteen years, so imagine my delight in being able to put a heroine, who's afraid to fly, into an undercover situation where she has to pretend to be an experienced flight attendant. I actually used a lot of things in this story that happened to me while on an airplane. It does bring a touch of realism to an otherwise fanciful tale. Keep that in mind when you're reading about the antics on the plane.

Happy reading,

Jordan Summers

JORDAN SUMMERS
Off Limits

TORONTO • NEW YORK • LONDON
AMSTERDAM • PARIS • SYDNEY • HAMBURG
STOCKHOLM • ATHENS • TOKYO • MILAN • MADRID
PRAGUE • WARSAW • BUDAPEST • AUCKLAND

If you purchased this book without a cover you should be aware that this book is stolen property. It was reported as "unsold and destroyed" to the publisher, and neither the author nor the publisher has received any payment for this "stripped book."

ISBN-13: 978-0-373-79387-7
ISBN-10: 0-373-79387-1

OFF LIMITS

Copyright © 2008 by Jordan Summers.

All rights reserved. Except for use in any review, the reproduction or utilization of this work in whole or in part in any form by any electronic, mechanical or other means, now known or hereafter invented, including xerography, photocopying and recording, or in any information storage or retrieval system, is forbidden without the written permission of the publisher, Harlequin Enterprises Limited, 225 Duncan Mill Road, Don Mills, Ontario M3B 3K9, Canada.

This is a work of fiction. Names, characters, places and incidents are either the product of the author's imagination or are used fictitiously, and any resemblance to actual persons, living or dead, business establishments, events or locales is entirely coincidental.

This edition published by arrangement with Harlequin Books S.A.

® and TM are trademarks of the publisher. Trademarks indicated with ® are registered in the United States Patent and Trademark Office, the Canadian Trade Marks Office and in other countries.

www.eHarlequin.com

Printed in U.S.A.

ABOUT THE AUTHOR

Jordan Summers is a former flight attendant with a penchant for huge bookstores and big dumb action movies. She prefers quiet dinners with friends over maddening crowds. She is happily married to her very own Highlander, and they split their time between two continents. Jordan is a member of the Romance Writers of America, Novelists Inc. and the Published Authors Network. She loves to hear from readers. You can reach Jordan at her Web site, www.jordansummers.com.

This book could not have happened without the support of my family. Mom, thanks for always believing in me. Dad, thanks for the sound advice.

To Si, thanks for showing me that romance heroes truly do exist. There is a piece of you in every hero that I write. I love you.

I'd like to thank Kathryn Lye for all her hard work, and thanks, too, to Jenny Rappaport. I would also like to thank the girls: Julie, Vivi, Charli, Sylvia, Kathy, Beth, Lynn and Terri.

Off Limits is dedicated to all the flight attendants in the world. I may have left the friendly skies, but I have not forgotten my fellow Sky Goddesses. You earn your wings every day. Keep flying high.

1

"I DON'T FLY," Delaney Carter stated as she stood in her group supervisor's utilitarian office. She glanced out the windows at the cloudless blue sky. The Phoenix sun glared back, baking the room and its two occupants as if they were a couple of Poppin' Fresh rolls. Sweat broke out across her brow and the muscles in her chest tensed at the thought of being airborne.

Roger McMillan cocked his corpulent head as if he hadn't heard her correctly. "I need hardly remind you about the geographic mobility agreement you signed."

She couldn't really blame him for being astonished. This was the first time she'd ever turned down an assignment, especially one of this magnitude, but it couldn't be helped. She'd managed to avoid air travel thus far and had no wish to end her no-fly streak. Delaney pulled at her starched shirt collar in an attempt to get more air into her lungs.

His penetrating brown eyes narrowed. Delaney fought the urge to shift under his steely regard. McMillan was a bull of a man—thick, balding and heavily muscled. It was difficult to tell where his neck ended and his barrel-shaped chest began. Most people simply followed the mustard stains on his tie.

"I don't have a problem with traveling, sir. I just prefer to do it on the ground."

"Are you afraid?" The last word slipped from his lips like a curse.

Delaney flushed, crossing her arms over her less-than-ample chest. She hated that she felt the need to defend her stance. She knew she was an exemplary agent without a single blemish in her file, and she intended for it to stay that way. The Bureau shouldn't hold her fear of flying against her, but Delaney knew it would, if she didn't take this mission.

"I asked you a question, Carter. Are you afraid to fly?"

"I didn't say that," she gritted out between clenched teeth. He knew damn well she was afraid to fly. He was just baiting her with the question.

"Well, then, what's the problem?" he bellowed, slapping an open folder down onto his oak desk.

"I'm not convinced things that heavy should be in the sky."

"What? Do you hear what you're saying? You do know what year it is, right?" He clutched his head in frustration. "Explain."

"I think the wings on the damn things are going to fall off midflight, and we'll plummet to the earth, bursting into a ball of flames."

"That's ridiculous! Besides, if it happened, you wouldn't feel a thing."

Delaney remained resolutely straight-faced. "Wow, that's comforting, and makes that whole burning-up part all better."

"You can check the attitude," he said, leveling his gaze.

"Yes, sir."

"Do you have any idea how many planes are in the sky at any given hour?"

Delaney took a deep breath, attempting to steady her nerves. It didn't matter if there were a million aircraft circling above their building right at this moment, as long as she didn't have to be on one of them. "The number of planes doesn't change how I feel about flying. I've read the stats. I understand the risks."

"So what's the problem with catching a flight tomorrow

morning?" Roger McMillan's Roman features solidified and his lips thinned, nearly disappearing into his mouth. He picked up a pen and began tapping an angry staccato beat against his desktop. "Do you want this assignment or not? Keep in mind, I'm not really asking. I went to a lot of trouble to get you here. Your father and I go way back, you know."

"I know, sir, and I appreciate that." Her father had phoned his old marine buddy McMillan to ensure she'd be assigned to his team. It was his way of keeping tabs on her without appearing to do so. At first, Delaney had resented the move, but later she'd discovered that McMillan was a fair man and didn't kowtow to anyone—and that included her father.

"Obviously you don't appreciate the opportunity enough to buck up and act like a GS-7 special agent. I don't have to remind you that some ATF agents wait their entire careers for an opportunity like this. We're talking about busting a major arms deal on U.S. soil. I would think, since you're finishing your master's and getting ready to upgrade, you'd jump at this chance."

Delaney heard McMillan's not so subtle subtext. *If you don't take this assignment, you can kiss your promotion goodbye.* He knew what this upgrade meant to her. She'd sacrificed everything this past year to achieve it...sleep, sex, even a wee bit of her sanity. She couldn't lose the promotion now. Not when she was so close.

"Who's behind the deal?" she asked.

"We don't know. That's one of the things you have to find out. You're going in as Delaney *Carson*. We figured we'd keep your new name as close to your old one as possible, so that it'd be easy to remember."

"Understood. What about carrying a weapon? I'm not going anywhere without my gun," she said, grasping at straws.

"We can arrange for you to get through security without being stopped, but you'll have to carry frangible rounds."

"Frangibles? They don't have stopping power worth a damn."

"Exactly. You need something with minimum penetration inside an airplane."

"But—"

He held up his hand. "Take it or leave it."

"I'll take it."

McMillan grinned. "Thought you might."

She toed the beige carpet under her sensible shoes. Sweat trickled beneath her barely there breasts. Delaney tugged at the sleeves of her navy suit jacket, wishing the air conditioner worked better. She'd give her left little piggy to be naked in a tub of ice right about now. "I appreciate the opportunity, sir. Any other time, the assignment wouldn't be a problem," she said, hoping he'd respond to reason.

"And this is *no* exception. We don't get to pick and choose our undercover assignments, Special Agent Carter. I need you to do this. Your ass isn't the only one on the line. I have Special-Agent-in-Charge Anderson breathing down my neck, as we speak. If the weapons are allowed to leave the West Coast, we may end up with another Waco on our hands—or worse."

"Yes, sir. I understand, but what you're asking me to do is humiliating. I'm a highly trained special agent for the Bureau of Alcohol, Tobacco, Firearms and Explosives, and you want me to pretend to be a stewardess."

"I believe they prefer the term *flight attendant* these days," he corrected.

"Stewardess, flight attendant, hostess, sky goddess, whatever. I'm not exactly known for my people skills."

"You definitely won't be voted Ms. Congeniality anytime soon." He laughed, then sobered. "Doesn't really matter, you fit the profile. Besides, the airline's willing to train you."

"Train me? How much can I learn in a week? Heck, it'll take me that long to deal with my fea—flying aversion."

"The airline assures me you'll be FAA-certified by the time you leave training. As for your aversion," he said, slamming the folder shut, "deal with it."

Delaney snorted. There was no way in hell she'd be ready in a week.

"That's an order, Special Agent Carter," he barked, leaving no room for argument. "We need Jack Gordon's expertise. Only a big fish could bait another in the nasty pond where we're going."

"But how do you know we're after a big fish?"

"Because only a major player could handle a shipment this size. We're talking enough to fill a couple of tractor trailers here. That's why we need Jack Gordon. He knows who brings weapons in. He's been in the business long enough that he can give us names and locations. We have to learn who's behind this new deal and stop them before they have a chance to sell the merchandise. If we had more time, we might do things differently, but we only have two weeks total to pull this all together before the window of opportunity closes. One of those you'll spend training. I hate to say it, but Gordon's our best hope."

"I thought the file said he was retired."

"Maybe, maybe not. The man is amazing at covering his tracks. We often had our suspicions about him, but could never prove a thing. Makes me wish he were one of my agents. Although if he were, Anderson would probably have a heart attack. He seems to have taken a special interest in the possibility of nailing Jack Gordon."

"Then why don't we pick him up? Sit on him for a while. Might be easier."

"We don't know for sure what he's been up to lately. The last thing we want him to do is get spooked and leave the country. He certainly has the assets to disappear if he wanted to. That's where you come in."

Delaney's brow furrowed. "I don't think I understand."

"Gordon has an eye for the ladies."

"Okay..."

McMillan stared at her, waiting for her to connect the dots. "You're a woman."

Heat filled Delaney's face until she was convinced her ears would blow off. "No disrespect, sir, but have you taken a good look at me lately? My body doesn't exactly scream 'come and get me.'" She'd had had her fair share of dates with fellow ATF agents, before she decided a year ago to focus on her studies. Everyone knew the score going into the relationship and there were no hard feelings when it ended. The job always came first, period. Delaney brushed a wisp of mousey hair out of her makeup-free face. "Besides," she continued, "I'd rather not get close to an arms dealer. The filth might rub off."

McMillan snorted. "You sound like Anderson. Guilty until proven innocent." Her boss took a deep breath. "We don't know that Jack Gordon is dirty."

She scoffed. "It comes with the job description." Something cold and unwelcome settled in Delaney's belly.

He straightened the documents in front of him, and then placed them in his outbox, before staring at her. "That remains to be seen. If you suspect Gordon is involved, I want you to pull out of the mission and call for backup. You have a week to get close to him. Make him trust you. Get him to cooperate. Is that going to be a problem given your family history?"

She stiffened. Delaney didn't need a reminder of what had occurred. Every time her sister Elaine phoned, she pictured the motorized wheelchair that was now her permanent home, the once athletic legs, shriveled from lack of use, and her parents' saddened expressions.

Delaney would never be the golden child of the family, no matter how many lives she saved, promotions she received, or bad guys she arrested. That was Elaine's position, or had been until some two-bit bandit shot her during her stint in the Peace Corps, leaving her paralyzed from the waist down.

Delaney had been trying to pick up the slack ever since. She knew all she wanted to know about gunrunners. "Is there a chance that Jack supplied guns to the rebels that shot my sister?"

McMillan looked decidedly uncomfortable. "Not that we can determine."

She felt her insides harden. "That's not a no."

He met her eyes. "I'll do some digging and see what I can find out. Until then, I expect you to do your job."

"Are you ordering me to protect him?"

McMillan shook his head. "His safety is not your concern. Your job is to collect the information. Anderson can send someone in to protect him if it comes to that. Just don't expect the cavalry to arrive quickly, since he considers Gordon expendable."

"Fat chance he's not involved." Delaney's stomach clenched. In her mind, she agreed with Special-Agent-in-Charge Anderson. Jack Gordon *was* expendable. Why worry about him, when he didn't concern himself over the many people his actions affected? "By nature, arms dealers are not trusting people. That's what keeps them alive. How am I supposed to get close to Gordon while I'm pretending to be a trolley-dolly?"

He arched a brow. "Use your imagination. Like I said, he fancies himself to be a ladies' man." McMillan slid a photo of her intended target across his desk. "He flies back and forth several times a week from Phoenix to Los Angeles. We've arranged for you to be on his flights."

"Great." Delaney glanced down. Her eyes locked on the picture and her breath caught in her lungs. Rich dark hair, dimples deep enough to swan-dive into and demanding blue eyes stared back at her, illuminating her current social drought as effectively as a spotlight. Why did the bad guys always have to look so damn good? She cleared her suddenly dry throat and met her group supervisor's gaze.

It took her a second to speak. "He's not what I expected. Doesn't exactly look like gun runner material, more like *GQ*." *Why did she suddenly sound breathless?*

"That's what makes him so dangerous. He's disarmingly average." McMillan placed the photo on top of the file.

Delaney studied at the picture. *Average* wouldn't be the word she would have chosen to describe Jack Gordon. Seductive, alluring, sex incarnate, maybe. Anything but average. Pity, seemed like such a waste of supreme male flesh to get him killed. "Explain to me again why we can't just arrest him. It would save us a lot of time and trouble." *And keep her from having to get close to him.*

"Because technically—" McMillan paused, frustration etching his features "—he hasn't done anything wrong."

Twenty-four hours later

"Heads down! Stay down! Heads down! Stay down! Heads down! Stay down!" The command slipped repeatedly from Delaney's numb lips without thought, just like the trainers said it would, the sadistic bastards. She swallowed her fear and the bile rising in her throat, and continued to shout.

The fuselage of the plane tilted and shook, attempting to catapult her and the flight attendant next to her out of their jumpseat. They hung on with the help of their four-prong seat belts and sheer determination. There was a reason why people shouldn't fly and this was it.

We're going to die.
We're going to die.

We're going to die.

The mantra played in Delaney's head, all the while the evacuation commands spewed out of her mouth like a fountain.

The cabin filled with gray smoke, lowering the visibility to a few feet. Her lungs burned as she braced for impact. Metal screeched. The overhead storage bins flew open, dropping luggage and clothing into the aisle. Time seemed to still. The light flickered off, plunging the cabin into darkness a second before the emergency exits illuminated.

People's screams ripped through Delaney, then slowly faded like a nightmare facing dawn. The passengers had their heads down, yet their frantic gazes continually sought hers for reassurance.

As if she could help them now. *We're all going to die.*

Delaney tried to smile, but it was difficult with her chin resting against her chest and her hands tucked firmly beneath her quaking thighs. She probably looked like the creature in *Alien* when its lips peeled back from its teeth as it prepared to strike. Goodness knows her breath made the same hissing sound with each exhalation.

"Heads down! Stay down! Heads down! Stay down! Heads down! Stay down!" Delaney choked, her throat burning from the fumes. She supposed now was not the time to remember that she hated to fly, hated most people and despised travel.

The Dallas flight attendant sitting next to her, who might as well have been named Barbie, considering the amount of silicone padding in her body, called out the exact same commands with less force and more twang. Her perfectly applied makeup and her sky-high blond hair seemed impervious to what was happening around them, unlike Delaney's limp brown hair, which had wilted an hour ago under the pressure. The disparity in hair color was only one more subtle sign that told Delaney she didn't fit in and shouldn't be here.

She stared at the attendant with a mixture of envy and horror. The woman was like a car bumper and flotation device all in one. Delaney debated for about a half second whether to use her as a buffer to break their fall.

This could not be happening.

Cold sweat broke out over Delaney's body and her stomach rolled, matching the rhythm of the plane. As if reading her earlier thoughts, the flight attendant beside her turned and smiled sweetly, almost blissful.

"We're going to be all right, sugar. Captain Martin has this big, bad tube under control."

Under control? She'd lost her friggin' mind. Delaney tried not to gape. *Was it wrong of her to hate the bitch?*

The plane jerked hard and bucked before skidding to a shuddering halt. Delaney pulled her hands out from under her legs and shook them to get the feeling back. A second later, Captain Martin gave the command to evacuate. Barbie was up and out of the jumpseat in seconds.

"Unfasten your seat belts! Unfasten your seat belts! Unfasten your seat belts!" Delaney shouted as she moved to the front entry door to assess the conditions outside the tiny scratched window. Heat filled the cabin. There was fire nearby, but it looked clear enough to open the door.

She slid her trembling fingers over the cool metal rotation handle. This was it. Freedom lay on the other side of the door. Delaney gave a glance over her shoulder. Barbie already had her door open and directed passengers to safety. The woman may look slow and talk slow, but she obviously moved with the speed of a cheetah.

Delaney lifted the handle. The entry door slid in a few inches, and then she pushed it out until it locked against the fuselage. "Come this way! This way out! Leave everything! Come this way! This way out! Leave everything!" she began to shout, a second before realizing the emergency evacuation slide hadn't inflated.

She cursed, not caring who heard her. Delaney reached down with both hands to pull the red inflation handle. The slide exploded to life just as someone bumped her from behind. Delaney shrieked, falling headfirst, end over end until the last five feet of slide remained. Her face slowed her progress from there.

She realized two things at that moment—the first was that rubber burned the same way a rug did, and the second was that a sufficient spackling of makeup can leave a skid mark five feet long and four inches wide.

Dazed and slightly confused, Delaney came to a halt at the bottom of the slide and had about a breath to roll out of the way before the passengers plowed into her.

They carried their luggage, shoes, seat bottom cushions and fire extinguishers, basically everything that wasn't nailed down.

Doesn't anyone listen to orders?

A shrill whistle blew behind her and Delaney stiffened. Like magic, the action came to a halt. She stumbled to her feet as the short, red-haired airline training instructor, Sandra Lopez, approached, holding her whistle in one hand and carrying her trusty stopwatch in the other.

"Not bad for your fifth try, Ms. Carson, but we're going to have to do it again. You understand," she said, shaking her head.

"Yeah, I understand." Delaney cringed inwardly.

Sandra glanced down at her watch. "This time it only took ten minutes. You're getting quicker," she said encouragingly. "All you have to do now is move a little faster, and remember to hold on to the handle inside the door, so you don't get pushed out of the airplane again. It's hard to evacuate an airplane from the ground." She grasped Delaney's chin, turning her face to the side.

Delaney winced.

"That'll heal in a couple of days. In the meantime, we'll cover it with makeup. You don't want to be caught without your face on." She winked, swirling a hand in front of her face for emphasis.

What was it with the women here and their makeup? The way Delaney saw it, she was one rouge stroke away from qualifying as a rodeo clown.

Delaney glanced at the instructor and fought the urge to shove the whistle down Sandra's throat. Somehow she had to shave eight or nine minutes off that time by the end of the week or this assignment was a bust. She'd told Group Supervisor McMillan she was the wrong woman for this job, but he hadn't believed her.

"Okay, let's do it again." Sandra's shout was followed by a quick whistle burst.

Delaney's shoulders scrunched to repel the sharp sound. Maybe Sandra's throat wasn't the right location for the whistle. She glanced down at the instructor's perky butt. Delaney's hands curled into fists to keep from ripping the whistle out of Sandra's fingertips.

This was a nightmare. A great big Texas-sized nightmare, and it was never going to end. It was like having to attend gym class in your underwear over and over again while everyone watched and snickered. She trudged back into the simulator plane, and slammed the forward entry door behind her.

Barbie stood in the galley, checking her makeup, and then reapplied her candy-apple red lipstick. She blew a kiss and waved at Captain Martin, before sitting on the jumpseat.

Delaney rolled her eyes, then strapped herself in. The passengers took their seats after closing the overhead bins in preparation for the next evacuation simulation.

"You can do it, sugar. Some people are just slower at

picking things up than others," Barbie drawled in her saccharine-sweet Texas accent, making Delaney feel like a bourbon-swilling bridge troll by comparison.

In that moment, Delaney was grateful she'd left her gun at home.

One week later...

DELANEY TOOK HER position at the front of the musty Boeing 737 aircraft bound for Los Angeles. *Where in the world was that smell coming from?* She sniffed the galley, covertly checked herself, then opened the lavatory door and nearly gagged as the putrid odor surrounded her. Eyes watering, she swung the door back and forth before shutting it to face the oncoming tide of people.

Mystery solved.

A sea of tidy blue seats winked at her as the passengers filed on board. Delaney stood with a smile glued on her face, saying hi at the same rate as she said bu-bye, while every fifth person stopped to ask her where they were supposed to sit.

For Pete's sake, sit anywhere, she thought, wondering when people lost the ability to read seat numbers on airline tickets.

That's what Delaney wanted to say, but she didn't. Instead, she said, "Your seat is past the bulkhead on the right side. Rows one through ten are reserved for first-class passengers only."

Without fail this speech caused their expressions to blank and their eyes to glaze over. Obviously, there was a limit to the amount of information the traveling public could accept at one time. "You're in seat seventeen A." Delaney's voice rose as she enunciated each word, then pointed to the back of the aircraft.

Now that she'd solved the passengers' problems, Delaney could address her current dilemma—how to make do overnight with no underwear except the thong on her body. How could she have forgotten to pack clean underwear? Her mother would be appalled.

She watched Jeremy Stevens, one of the senior flight attendants assigned to work with her, shuffle past a woman carrying a huge roller bag down the narrow aisle. She struggled to put the bag into the overhead bin, almost dropping it on the head of a passenger who sat in a nearby seat.

"Excuse me, sir. Could you help me lift this?" the woman asked, plopping the bag at Jeremy's feet without waiting for an answer.

Jeremy beamed, then glanced at the bag in the aisle. "I'm sorry, but if you can't lift it, then it's not really a carry-on, now is it?" he said, then proceeded to the back of the aircraft for a baggage claim ticket.

Delaney covered her mouth and giggled, turning away so the customers in the cabin couldn't see her. Leave it to Jeremy to say something like that. In the few short days she'd worked for the airline, Delaney realized some attendants could get away with saying anything. She, unfortunately, wasn't one of them. Her file already held ten customer complaints and counting, and she was only on her second trip.

The woman continued to struggle. Delaney tried to ignore her, but her conscience wouldn't allow it. Without looking at the oncoming passengers, she held up her hand and stopped the flow of traffic, then proceeded down the aisle.

"Here, let me help you with that," she said, hoisting the unusually heavy roller bag over her head. What was the woman carrying? Bricks? The suitcase wobbled, threatening to fall. Delaney's fingers slipped, tipping the bag dangerously toward the seated passengers. She clawed at the material in an attempt to regain control, but it was too late.

Heat enveloped her as a warm, hard body pressed into her

back, cradling her hips and butt intimately. A firm hand shot out, gripping the side of the bag in time to prevent it from falling.

"Looks like you could use a little help." A rich, seductive French-roast voice poured over her from behind.

Delaney closed her eyes and trembled under the impact, before turning to face her savior. "Thanks for the—" was all she managed to get out, before she gasped as if she'd been kicked in the chest by an angry mule. Her eyes locked on to the man in front of her. He hefted the bag into the bin as if it weighed no more than goose down.

Jack Gordon stood in the aisle, smiling wide enough to display those dazzling dimples. His midnight blue gaze casually caressed her body, before traveling back to her face. How many women had fallen for that innocent expression? The airplane seemed to close in around them, or maybe it was just her.

Delaney quivered under his silent regard. She wished she could say it was out of fear, but it wasn't. Fear didn't make your nipples hard or your body ache.

Heat infused her face and her mind blanked like some kind of bobble-head doll. So this was the man she was supposed to get close to? Hell, the picture might as well have been his driver's license photo for all the justice it did him. McMillan was right. Jack Gordon was dangerous, but for different reasons than he'd implied.

He wore a black suit jacket over a pair of faded blue jeans, pulling off the casual chic look effortlessly. His dark hair curled seductively over the collar, caressing the silk fabric. A white T-shirt molded his broad chest, nipping in at his tight stomach.

He wouldn't win any bodybuilding contests, but the man was toned, which meant he stayed active. Delaney didn't want to think about what he did to keep that body. She glanced at his feet. His Ferragamos looked to be about a size twelve. She groaned inwardly as her thoughts dropped into the gutter.

"If you'll excuse me, I have to get back to my boarding position. Thanks for the help." She stepped forward. Their bodies brushed as she squeezed past him, sending a ripple of awareness through her. Delaney prayed that he didn't notice.

Jack's lips quirked and he looked as if he were going to say more as she passed, but instead he retrieved his luggage. Shaken, she returned to the front of the plane.

Gordon strode down the aisle to his first-class seat. Loose limbs and fluid movements gave Delaney the impression he was relaxed, but her years of training told her that he projected what he wanted people to see. It was disarmingly effective.

For a few seconds, he'd managed to sway her with his casual charm. Dangerous, dangerous man. Suddenly playing Mr. Helpful, she watched Jeremy brighten, then offer to take Gordon's jacket and hang it in a nearby closet reserved for flight attendants only.

Was it her imagination or had Jack Gordon's shoulders expanded?

Carnal thoughts rushed through her mind as she envisioned his bare chest flexing under her fingertips, the smooth glide of skin brushing skin. Jeremy rushed forward, his face bright with excitement, effectively disbursing her salacious fantasy.

"Goodness, girl, did you see the heavenly creature seated in eight A? I think I'm in love." He raised his hand to his heart and pretended to swoon.

"Yeah, I noticed him," she said, clearing her throat. "Kind of hard not to."

She glanced into the cabin as Jack looked up. Their eyes met and held. Delaney felt the spark all the way to her toes. It crackled like static electricity through her nerve endings. She shouldn't be attracted to this man. He represented everything she despised. He had to be dirty. All she had to do was find the proof. Delaney relaxed a little as the last thought crossed her mind. She could do this.

Jeremy preened. "That man is so hot. You'd have to be dead to miss him."

"I know." Delaney couldn't seem to tear her gaze away. Until she uncovered proof, getting close to Jack Gordon wouldn't exactly be a hardship. All she had to do was keep things strictly business. Why did that suddenly seem so difficult?

Jeremy peeked over her shoulder. "I could just eat him up." His jaw snapped shut and he smacked his lips for emphasis.

Delaney chuckled, and turned to look at Jeremy. "I hate to disappoint you, but I don't think he's gay."

Jeremy arched one perfectly sculpted brow and tugged at his crisp navy uniform. "Who cares? Give me an hour and I'll turn him."

It took a second for Delaney to register what he'd said, then she burst out laughing. Jeremy certainly made the job entertaining, and she was beyond grateful after the hellish week she'd spent in Dallas training. She glanced around the corner of the galley wall once again.

Jack Gordon stared directly at her, amusement dancing over his provocative features. Her heart moshed against her ribs. She took a deep breath and then let it out slowly. "He's merely an assignment," she murmured to herself. *Expendable*...Delaney choked, then quickly ducked back into the galley.

"Do I look okay?" Jeremy asked as he combed his receding hair and straightened his tie.

"You look fine," she told him, reaching out to stop him in his tracks.

"What's the matter?" He frowned. "Does my breath stink?" He blew into his cupped hand and sniffed.

"No, it's fine."
"Then let me go, my prince is waiting."
"Sorry to do this to you, buddy, but this one's all mine."

2

DELANEY STROLLED down the aisle, shutting overhead bins. Her mind accepted then rejected various ideas of how to approach Jack Gordon. Time was running out. There was barely a week left for her to get the information she needed and stop the shipment from being sold. She also needed to get close enough to plant the bug McMillan had given her. Delaney reached Jack's row and glanced down at his lap. He held a Zero Halliburton aluminum briefcase in his hands.

"Would you like me to stow that for you, sir?" she asked, hoping he gave it to her so she could search the contents.

"That won't be necessary." His fingers flexed and he clutched the case tighter.

Delaney's eyes narrowed. What was so important inside the case that he didn't want to give it up? "FAA regulations state that all carry-on items must be stowed for taxi, takeoff and landing. If you can't fit the bag under the seat in front of you, I'll have to find a spot in an overhead bin or check it."

He smiled, but his grip tightened almost imperceptibly. "I'll make it fit," he said, carefully sliding the briefcase forward under the seat in front of him.

Delaney opened her mouth to say more, but the captain took that moment to announce that the aircraft had been cleared for departure. "Flying time from Phoenix to Los Angeles will be one hour and twenty minutes. Flight attendants take your seats."

She returned to her jumpseat and began to strap in. Her fingers trembled as she slipped the flat ends into the buckles and pulled the shoulder straps tight. The engines roared and the plane readied for takeoff. Delaney felt the color leech from her skin as they picked up speed.

She started to whisper the mantra she'd created in class as the front end lifted, slowly followed by the tail section.

"We're all going to die."

"We're all going to die."

"We're all going to die."

There was something perversely helpful about it.

They hit an air pocket and Delaney braced. The plane rocked back and forth like a seesaw, while the pilots struggled to steady it. Delaney followed every movement in her mind, knowing it could be her last.

"What's happening?" she asked Jeremy as full-blown panic set in.

"A little turbulence."

"I can feel that, but why isn't it stopping?" Delaney shushed him, before he could answer. "I think I heard something. Was that an engine stalling? Aren't they supposed to hum?"

Jeremy blinked, then furrowed his brow. "When did you say you finished training?"

"Two days ago."

"I suppose that explains it," he said.

"What?"

"The engines are fine. I think the pilots would've notified us if we needed to prepare the cabin for an emergency landing. They're funny that way."

The aircraft gave one final jerk, then calmed. A ding sounded a moment later followed by an announcement from the cockpit.

"We're finally out of the rough air, folks, so we've turned

off the fasten seat belt sign. You're free to move about the cabin, but we ask that while you're seated please keep your seat belts at least loosely fastened."

Jeremy leaned in close to her ear. "Next time, you might want to keep your expression calm and try not to say 'we're all going to die' quite so loud. You're scaring the passengers." He shook his head and unfastened his seat belt, muttering something about rookie flight attendants under his breath.

JACK GORDON covertly watched the female flight attendant at the front of the cabin. Light brown hair and chocolate-colored eyes dominated her girl-next-door features. There was nothing special about her appearance, but Jack could still feel the scalding impression her round bottom had left on the front of his jeans.

His entire body had tensed in awareness and he hadn't relaxed yet. For that reason alone, she fascinated him. Long pale fingers pulled at the seat belts, pressing her small breasts together, until she managed to free herself. He followed the delicate rise and fall of her chest, trying to imagine what he'd find if he peeled back her uniform shirt. Lacy material, pale globes, taunt peaks. He swallowed hard, his throat suddenly constricted.

Her brown eyes widened with each bump of the aircraft. At one point, she'd actually clutched her heart and paled. It was as if she'd never flown before. Her actions screamed *newbie*, but he noticed something else that he'd never witnessed in an airline attendant: fear.

She was doing her best to hide it, but the emotion remained. Jack had the overwhelming urge to go to the front of the plane and hold her, reassure her that everything was going to be all right. He had no idea where these protective urges came from, but there was no denying they were there. He forced himself to stay put.

An airline attendant who was afraid to fly? Jack shook his

head at the crazy thought. He was probably reading too much into her expression.

She rose and walked into the galley, head held high and shoulders back, leaving no indication that the fear had ever been there. The gentle sway of her lean hips accented her bottom. The material of her uniform cupped the soft arc lovingly. Jack gripped the armrest, his thumbs stroking the sides as if he longed to touch the attendant.

He shook himself. Why was he acting like this when he had women on speed dial available? He wasn't hard up or desperate. Maybe he'd grown tired of the same ol' same ol'.

Lately, Jack's thoughts had turned to settling down. It wasn't as if his biological clock was ticking. He had plenty of time to find the right woman. He needed someone who could look beyond his money. Someone he didn't have to lie to about his past.

Jack had grown tired of the lies a long time ago, but he'd learned the hard way not to tell the whole truth. Women of quality did not want to date ex-arms dealers. He'd retired and moved onto a safer profession of buying and selling exquisite art, but his present occupation didn't eliminate his past or diminish the restlessness he felt.

Not that he had any plans to date this flight attendant. He was too busy moving his art collection from his California home to his new Phoenix digs to get involved. Maybe once that was taken care of, he'd reconsider.

Despite those reasons, Jack couldn't deny his interest in this particular woman. She made him burn, when others couldn't produce a spark.

DELANEY STOCKED the beverage cart. The plane continued to climb, but if she didn't start now she wouldn't finish her drink service in time to plant a bug in Jack Gordon's suit coat.

From his earlier behavior with his luggage, she was convinced he was up to something. The question was what? It wasn't as if he'd walked on with a bag full of weapons. Security would've frowned upon that.

She glanced around the corner of the galley wall. He was still staring in her direction. The man hadn't taken his eyes from her since she'd strapped into her jumpseat. His attention made Delaney's skin itch and her nerves tingle. *Was it hot in here?* She wiped her brow. She couldn't allow him to rattle her. She'd get caught if she did.

Delaney didn't want to think about how his gaze made her body ache, her senses more alert. At one point, she'd known he was staring at her breasts. She could still feel the heat his look generated.

Feelings have no room on this mission, she reminded herself.

She shut the beverage cart door and pushed it into the aisle. It was like trying to steer a possessed grocery cart with four bum wheels. Delaney swore the metal contraption would be the death of her, if the plane didn't take care of her first. The cart shimmied and squeaked row by row as she worked her way down the aisle, pouring drinks for the first-class passengers.

"Can I get you something to drink?" Delaney asked.

"What do you have?" the man in row four countered.

The cart jiggled. "Not a lot of time, sir," she said, glancing down the aisle at Jeremy, who was slowly working his way toward her. She'd never get her drinks done at this rate.

The man's eyebrows rose to his hairline, before he eventually asked for a soda.

Delaney had made it two more rows into her service when a call button went off behind her. She turned to see a woman raise her glass in the air. "I'd like another," the woman called out.

"I'll be right with you, ma'am," she said, turning back to finish her service.

The woman swirled the ice in her glass, then shook it like a pair of dice in a Yahtzee cup. Delaney gripped the cart until her knuckles turned white. *Don't do it, lady.* "Yes?" She swung around to the woman again, a smile painted on her face.

"I said I'd like another drink."

Delaney took a deep breath and silently counted to ten. "I heard you, ma'am, but I have to serve the rest of my section before I hand out seconds."

"I want another drink now!" The woman reached for the call button and pressed it repeatedly like a clockwork monkey. Delaney set the brake on her cart. It threatened to roll down the aisle. She stepped harder until she heard a faint click. The cart stayed put.

Delaney strode toward the woman, picturing how she planned to rip her fingernails off, then pluck her nose hairs out one by one.

Undoubtedly sensing the woman's impending demise, Jeremy rushed forward past Delaney before she could reach the woman. He stepped in front of her, blocking Delaney from her destination. "Watch and learn," he said, then faced the disgruntled passenger. "Is there a problem here?"

"She won't give me another drink." The woman pointed at Delaney with her middle finger, using the hand that gripped her cup.

"Ma'am, you'd better put that finger away." Delaney stepped forward.

"I said I'd handle this." Jeremy shot Delaney a warning glance. "I believe she's still serving her first round, ma'am."

The woman quickly jerked sideways to glare at them. "I don't care what in the hell she's doing. I said I want a drink and I want it now."

Jeremy's demeanor changed subtly. He straightened his shoulders and stared down at the woman over his generous nose. "Honey, let me tell you something. I want a lot of things, but I don't always get them."

"But—"

"I'm not finished," he said, cutting her off. "There's only room for one queen on this aircraft and it ain't you." Jeremy slapped the call button off, and then proceeded down the aisle to finish his beverage service.

The woman gaped at his retreating back in stunned disbelief, before turning forward in her seat. The passengers around her snickered behind their in-flight magazines.

Hands sticky from soda, Delaney proceeded with her beverage service. She reached Jack Gordon's row and paused, locking the cart in place. "Can I get you something to drink, sir?"

Jack smiled. "Tomato juice, please."

Her heart kicked up a notch as she tore her gaze away from his face. She grabbed a plastic cup and plunged it into the ice bag sitting on top of her cart with a little too much gusto. The cart shook and moved forward an inch.

"Stay," she said, daring the trolley to move—which was a mistake.

Light turbulence bounced the occupants of the cabin. *Please make it stop.* Her heart thudded wildly and her palms started to sweat. The captain made an unintelligible announcement and the seat belt sign came back on. Fingers trembling, Delaney poured some of the tomato juice into the cup, using her wrist to brace herself on the handle of the beverage cart.

The plane climbed steadily toward a higher altitude. She turned to hand the drink to Jack Gordon. He reached for it, but couldn't quite grasp it. Delaney stretched sideways, accidentally bumping the cart with her hip. The beverage trolley began to roll…and roll…and roll.

With an open can of tomato juice in one hand and a full glass in the other, Delaney watched in horror as the beverage cart picked up speed, rumbling down the aisle like an avalanche of steel. She dropped the juice onto what she thought was the tray table. It landed with a thick *ker-plunk* in Jack's lap, covering his jeans in red goo.

He yelped. "What the—"

"Look out," she screamed, ignoring the man beside her.

Jeremy leapt out of the way, but somehow managed to land in the lap of a hunky California surfer dude. The cart roared past him, but he didn't appear to be in any hurry to stand. He'd thrown his arms around the man's neck, brushing his sun-bleached shoulder-length hair away from his tie-dyed T-shirt.

"Barbie, look out!" That wasn't her given name, but since Delaney couldn't bring herself to call the doll-like woman Barbara, Barbie would have to do.

With the grace of a ninja, the blond flight attendant spun, sticking her high-heeled foot out in front of her to stop the cart dead. She glanced up, brushing a stray hair away from her flawless face. The cabin erupted in applause, before quieting to stare at Delaney.

Delaney raised her hand in apology. The blonde shrugged before continuing to serve drinks as if nothing happened. Heat infused Delaney's face as she glanced at Jack.

"I'm sorry, sir. I have a cleaning slip in the closet. If you come with me to the front of the aircraft, I'll try to get that stain out. I don't suppose you brought a change of clothing aboard."

He shook his head and laughed. "I've never seen a runaway beverage cart. What do you do for an encore?"

"Stick around and find out."

"Somehow I think it would be worth it." He grinned then. "I guess I should have ordered water," he said, glancing down. He dabbed at the tomato juice ineffectively with his napkin.

"Let me get that cleaning slip. If you want to make your way to the front of the cabin, I'll be right with you," Delaney repeated, moving to the closet where Jeremy had stored the jacket.

She plucked a cleaning slip from the stack situated at the top of the closet on a small shelf, then began to search the clothing for seat numbers. Jeremy, the flirt, had been busy. There were at least nine jackets hanging in the closet. Despite that fact, it only took her a second to find Jack's suit coat. She glanced down the aisle to ensure he wasn't watching, then stuck a pinlike tracking device into the lining of his jacket.

Delaney shut the closet door. It was done. Now she'd be able to track Mr. Gordon once he reached Los Angeles. She tucked the cleaning slip into her pocket and walked to the forward galley. Jack stood behind the galley wall out of view of the main cabin, dripping fat red drops onto the burnt orange rubber floor.

"A little club soda will take that right out." She opened a hatch in the galley and plucked a can of club soda out of its hiding place. "I never knew what a miracle product this was," she said, rambling like an idiot.

Relax, no one in the cabin can see you. You've worked undercover before. This isn't your first day on the job. So what if all the cases had been minor.

It didn't matter that this was the biggest case she had ever been assigned or that her promotion and the well-being of who knew how many innocent citizens were riding on her success. Her duty was to get next to Jack Gordon and she had...sort of.

Delaney walked around Jack, careful not to touch him, not because she was worried about getting tomato juice on her uniform, but because she didn't like the feelings he invoked when they touched.

She grabbed a handful of paper towels, and turned the galley lights on bright, so she could see what she was doing. It was worse than she thought. A massive spot covered Jack's jeans from groin to midthigh. Delaney took a deep breath and blew it out.

"This is going to be a bit cold, but it can't be helped," she warned.

"Believe me, it already is." He laughed, a rich robust sound that sent tremors racing through her body.

"Stand still."

"What are you going to—" The words died in Jack's throat and his blue eyes widened in comprehension.

It didn't occur to Delaney that there was a problem until she slowly dropped to her knees and came face to zipper with one *very* impressive Jack Gordon.

JACK'S MIND CEASED to function as the flight attendant dropped to her knees before him. The cold he'd felt only moments ago faded into a slow burn that seemed to rise at the speed at which her slender hands made contact with his jeans.

He spied the name on her wings. Delaney. Pretty name for such a... He revised his earlier assessment of her. She was still the girl next door, but there was something alluring about her doe-like eyes. They were luminous and shimmering like the ocean at night on a full moon. Her lips were neither plump nor thin, but somewhere in between.

He wondered just how much they'd swell if someone kissed her senseless. Despite some trembling, her hands continued to work, patting his jeans with club soda. Earlier she'd deliberately avoided his gaze, which told him that she wasn't exactly immune in the situation.

The slow graceful movements she made while stroking his inner thigh had Jack thinking of where else he'd like to have her caress. "I'm Jack Gordon," he said, clearing his throat and willing his shaft to remain flaccid, which was as effective as spitting in the wind to put out a forest fire.

"Delaney Car— Carson," she rasped.

Her eyes rounded more, if it were even possible. Hand raised, she hesitated an inch away from his leg, her gaze darting from the wet spot to his growing need and back again. Jack watched her pink tongue dart out of her mouth to moisten her lower lip and had to fight back a groan.

He nearly choked as he spoke. "I think you missed a spot." Jack pointed to a spot above his knee.

Her mouth dropped open and Jack knew he was a goner.

"Oh, my, what are you doing?" Jeremy asked as he rounded the corner into the galley.

"I'm cleaning his pants," Delaney said as if that should be obvious.

"Is that what they're calling it these days? I could've sworn the new term was sexual…harassment." Jeremy cocked his head and arched a brow. "I used the old 'cleaning someone's pants' as an excuse five years ago. It didn't work then, either. I'll leave you to it." He turned and left the galley, laughing as he walked away.

"I'll get the rest," Jack said, snatching the paper towels out of her hands and striding into the lavatory. He shut the door behind him and leaned against it for support. The teeth of his zipper bit into his tender flesh as he attempted to adjust the weight of his arousal.

What in the hell had just happened? He wasn't some kind of randy teenager who got easily turned on by sexual innuendo. He'd come close to losing control with a woman he shouldn't even be attracted to. Yet, she'd done more for his libido in a few minutes than the last five women he'd dated in the past year.

He shook his head and pressed the tap on the water dispenser. Jack splashed the cool liquid over his face, then braced his hands on the side of the sink, curling his fingers as he stared into the mirror. Droplets ran down his cheeks onto his shirt. The blue of his eyes was damn near black with need.

Jack's hands trembled as he pulled out a fresh paper towel and dried his flushed face. He reminded himself that until he finished his move, he didn't need any female complications. Once he settled into life in Paradise Valley and got his bearings with the greater Phoenix area, maybe he'd give Delaney a call. He knew that made perfect sense and was absolutely the right move to make. So why was he taking out his wallet to retrieve one of his business cards?

3

DELANEY THUMBED the white card with gold embossed lettering that Jack Gordon handed her as he'd left the aircraft. Maybe her luck was turning. She and her crew had caught the shuttle outside of Terminal 1, riding the bus to the Doubletree Guest Suites in Santa Monica. Delaney knew her room would be set up for surveillance. She'd track Jack from there and decide her next move.

The Doubletree Guest Suites looked like any other midsize hotel. Situated four blocks from the beach and right next to the Santa Monica Freeway, the hotel couldn't be in a better location for her purposes.

She tipped the shuttle driver and strode into the lobby. A huge Native-American basket-weave design greeted her as she half rolled and half dragged her bag over to the front desk. Had she somehow pissed off the wheel gods without knowing it? A sealed envelope was waiting. McMillan had been busy, while she worked her flight. Delaney glanced over to make sure that Jeremy and Barbie were still preoccupied with the car rental forms, before snatching the envelope off the counter. She shoved it in her bag upon their approach.

"Hey, we've rented a car and are going for dinner and drinks, care to join us?"

Delaney looked at her crew. Despite working with them over the past few days, she didn't feel as if she belonged. Her real job kept her alienated and she liked it that way...or had. Other than the guys she'd dated, she never really hung out with her coworkers socially at the ATF. Working for the airline, where employees routinely hugged each other and met for meals, made that fact painfully obvious.

"No, thank you," she replied. "I'm kind of beat. I think I'll go to bed early."

Jeremy glanced at his watch. "It's only six."

"I know, but I'm still getting used to this schedule." That wasn't exactly a lie. She'd never been so tired in her life and she'd worked longer hours at ATF.

"Okay, see you tomorrow." They left, making plans for the night ahead.

Delaney plucked her key from the front desk clerk's fingers with a quick thank-you, and walked across the lobby to the elevator doors. She could hear Jeremy's and Barbie's laughter fading as the door shut. A twinge of envy hit her, but she brushed it away. She didn't have time to socialize. She was on duty.

A ding foretold the glass elevator's arrival. Delaney stepped inside. The clear wall gave her a view of the ocean as the sun set over Santa Monica. She allowed herself to relax and enjoy the view for a moment. It was easy to forget how beautiful the ocean was while living in a landlocked state like Arizona.

She had the overwhelming urge to throw her things in her room and then go dip her toes into the cool water. Delaney shook herself. She wasn't here on vacation. This was an assignment. She turned away from the view and waited for the elevator doors to open.

Delaney stepped into a deserted hall when she reached the fourth floor. Her room sat at the end of the corridor next to the exit. Just in case she needed to vacate in a hurry. She slipped her key into the lock and opened the door.

The taupe floors and peach-striped walls of her hotel room

greeted her. She pulled her roller-bag inside and locked the door. Lonely silence enveloped her. She sighed. It was just like home, except she probably wouldn't be able to sleep in the unfamiliar surroundings.

A laptop sat on a nearby desk next to a portable GPS unit. A set of rental car keys lay to the right of them. She knew bullets for her gun would be in the desk drawer. The Bureau wouldn't want her going into the field with frangible rounds. She unstrapped her ankle holster and popped the clip out of her SIG Sauer, replacing it with 9 mm rounds of ammo.

Delaney turned on the laptop and waited for it to boot. As long as Jack Gordon still had his jacket on, she'd be able to track where he went.

She grabbed the envelope that McMillan had left for her and tore it open. Inside was the photo of a geeky college kid. At least that's what she thought at first glance. Upon further examination, Delaney noticed lines bracketing his cruel mouth and the coldness of his eyes.

Delaney flipped the photo over. The name David Rico was splashed across the back. Beneath it was a notation in McMillan's masculine scrawl.

Secondary contact—small-time dealer.

Was she supposed to look for David Rico now? Should she drop surveillance on Jack Gordon? Delaney flipped open her phone. Her finger hovered above the number she used to speed-dial McMillan. She was about to press it, when the screen on her computer glowed to life. A map popped up, showing a red blip in Marina Del Rey, fifteen minutes away from her hotel. What was Jack doing in there, when he lived in Malibu?

She flipped the phone shut and changed out of her uniform quickly into a pair of faded jeans and a white blouse. Delaney slipped her ankle-high boots on, shoving her ID, credit card and cash into her pocket, before strapping on her pistol. She snatched the portable GPS unit off the desk, then pocketed her keys and raced out the door. If she hurried, she might be able to catch him before he left.

JACK PULLED IN TO the parking lot of Jerry's Famous Deli. He couldn't seem to shake the feeling that he was being watched. He glanced around the area, slowly scanning the parked cars. A flash of movement brought his gaze back to a rented blue Chevy sedan. Was it his imagination or had someone ducked the second he looked over that way?

He knew it. Someone was following him. His gut never lied and had kept him alive on more than one occasion. Too bad it hadn't helped on his final arms sale.

Hell, his guns had killed so many. He might as well have pulled the trigger himself. It would've been a lot more humane than what his last buyers had done. A shudder ran through his body as he recalled the acrid smell of burning flesh. He'd warned the neighboring villagers of the approaching threat, then walked away from his job and his old life, vowing never to return. He'd been too late to save them.

Jack's gut clenched as he slipped his Glock into his shoulder holster, pulling his jacket down over it before exiting his Lexus. Some habits died harder than others. He strode to the front door. His pace was even as he watched for more movement out of the corner of his eye.

As soon as he'd opened the door and stepped inside the deli, Jack made his way toward the back of the restaurant, ignoring his hunger and the delicious aromas wafting in the air.

His stomach knotted as his mind raced through various scenarios. Was it someone from his past looking to even a score? Another government agent out to bust him? How many times did he have to tell those people that he was a legit dealer, before they quit harassing him? He'd been out of the business for over a year, at least.

Jack walked through the kitchen and left via the back door, ducking as he reached the cars. He crept forward, slowly making his way to the parked Chevy. A horn blared nearby. His heart lurched, but he kept moving. Jack ventured a glance or two at the driver, but with the oncoming darkness all he could see were shadows.

Standing one car away, Jack stepped behind the blue sedan. He sprinted the remaining feet to the driver's door, his hand resting on the grip of the gun beneath his jacket.

Delaney gasped, swinging wildly with one hand, nearly clocking Jack in the face. She bent at the waist, reaching for something near the floorboard, then suddenly stopped as recognition dawned.

"You scared the daylights out of me," she said, pressing a hand to her heart.

He released his weapon and casually pulled out a handkerchief from his inside pocket as if that was what he'd been reaching for all along. He wiped his dry brow, then shoved the white cotton back inside. "What are you doing here?" Jack knew he was yelling, but it pissed him off that she'd come so close to getting herself shot.

"I—I was hungry." She glanced at the front of Jerry's Famous Deli, and then back at him.

"You were watching me," he accused, refusing to let her change the subject. "What are you doing in a rental car?"

Delaney took a deep breath and straightened her shoulders, then allowed them to drop. She met his gaze head-on. Jack's heart kicked hard in his chest and he felt himself melt under her regard. "I saw you after I pulled in. There is a difference between seeing and watching. As for the car, I wasn't about to rely on the taxi service in Los Angeles and the Getty Museum is located a little too far away to walk."

"I thought you said that you were hungry." His gaze narrowed.

"I am. I planned to eat first, then go to the museum."

His brow furrowed. "That still doesn't explain why you ducked."

"You saw that?"

He rested his palm on the roof of her car. "Yes, I saw that."

She blushed in the most adorable way, before glancing at her hands. "I didn't want you to think I was following you, especially after you gave me your card. I don't usually date passengers. Most flight attendants don't."

Jack's lips twitched. "Usually? Does that mean you were going to call?"

She looked past him at the deli's front doors. "Maybe."

Jack smiled then. He couldn't help it. She looked like a kid who'd just got caught with a mouthful of chocolate. He reached for her door handle and pulled. The door opened wide. "Since you're here, you could always join me for dinner."

"I don't know if that would be such a good idea."

"I think I owe you, for scaring you half to death. Most women would've done a lot more than gasp." He stilled as he considered her unusual reaction.

"I GUESS I'M NOT like most women." Delaney had heard those words so many times in her life that she now believed them. *Women don't try to carry all the groceries at once. Women don't like to shoot guns. Women don't enjoy Israeli Krav Maga fighting classes. Women don't join the ATF and they certainly don't become field agents.*

And of course the pièce de résistance—*Why can't you be more like your sister?* She couldn't be angry with her parents. Delaney knew they were only trying to protect her.

It was bad enough having one daughter incapacitated. They didn't need two.

Jack waited for her to undo her seat belt, then he helped her out of the car. Delaney took a couple of deep breaths, smoothing her jeans to cover any trace of her ankle holster. She didn't want to think about how close she'd come to shooting him.

"I kind of like that you aren't like most women. It makes you unique," he said, allowing his gaze to rake her as she hit the button on her remote to set the car alarm. "Shall we?"

Delaney nodded as he led her into the restaurant.

"I hope you're hungry."

"Why?" she asked, glancing at the huge array of items behind the glass counter as they entered the deli.

Jack grinned. "You'll see."

"That sounds ominous."

"It's a warning," he said with a wink.

"Perhaps I should warn you first."

He tilted his head to peer at her. "About what?"

"My appetite." She smiled. "I'm a hearty eater. In my family, you had to clean your plate and I was known as the bottomless pit."

Jack laughed. "Sounds like the house I grew up in, but good luck doing that here."

A hostess seated them after a short five-minute wait. The waitress, a woman named Lisa, who had enough piercing to be classified as a lightning rod, took their order and set off for the kitchen. A minute later a busboy came buy and dropped a basket of bagel chips onto the table along with green tomatoes and pickles.

Delaney picked up a cinnamon-raisin chip and started munching.

"I wouldn't do that if I were you," Jack teased. "You're going to need all the room you can get."

"I'll take my chances."

"When the food arrives, remember those famous last words."

Delaney's eyes nearly popped out of her head as the waitress placed the pastrami sandwich in front of her. There must have been some mistake. She'd only ordered a sandwich, not a platter. How was she going to take a bite out of this thing? It was over four inches thick, not counting the bread.

Jack watched her as he bit into his roast beef. "Doing all right there, tiger?"

"I'm managing," she said, devising a plan of attack.

"The best approach is to dig in."

Delaney lifted half the sandwich and tried to take a bite. Her mouth wouldn't open wide enough. Jack started to laugh.

The sound washed over Delaney, easing the tension in her muscles, while drawing her near. "It's not funny."

"Yes, it is," he said, wiping the side of his mouth with his napkin.

Delaney followed his movements, her gaze straying to his lips and dimpled cheeks. The man truly was *GQ* gorgeous. Would he kiss as good as he looked? Whoa! There would be no kissing on this assignment. It didn't matter that the man's mouth looked like it had been created for oral gratification. She tilted her head higher so that she was no longer staring at his sensual lips.

His blue eyes twinkled as if he knew exactly what she'd been thinking. Delaney ignored him and concentrated on her food. She flipped off the top piece of bread and dug into her sandwich with her knife and fork. The pastrami practically melted in her mouth.

"Mmm...this is great," she said around bites.

Jack nodded. "I know. I like to come to Jerry's at least a couple of times a month. They have the best matzo ball soup you'll ever taste."

"I'll have to remember that for next time," she said, sipping her Coke. The bubbles tickled her nose and she snuffled.

"Are we going to do this again sometime?" His voice held an edge of eagerness that surprised her.

No, absolutely not. He could be the reason that Elaine would spend the rest of her life in a chair, her mind screamed, disappointing her body. Delaney knew that no matter what happened there was no chance that she and Jack would end up together. You can't build a lasting relationship on a foundation of lies. Not that she'd actually considered having a relationship with Jack. She was simply caught up in the moment.

Delaney shrugged and said, "Let's see how this meal goes first."

Jack's lips parted in a knowing smile, causing Delaney's stomach to flutter. "I suppose that's good enough for now."

"SO TELL ME ABOUT yourself," Jack encouraged, wanting to know more about her. She was a bit of a puzzle to him. Her actions said one thing, while her expressions and words said another. He wondered which was the true Delaney and decided he was interested enough to find out.

"Not much to tell," she said, wetting her lips and shifting nervously in her seat.

He noted her tongue's movements and felt his arousal grow. When he met her eyes, awareness blazed between them, then her brown gaze fell away from his face. She glanced out the window at the parking lot as if it was the most fascinating thing she'd ever seen.

"I thought most people enjoyed talking about themselves," he said.

"Like *I said*, I'm not like most people." A strange vulnerability overtook her features.

Jack reached out and brushed a crumb off her cheek. Delaney swallowed hard and the pulse jumped in her throat. He smiled to himself. Jack had never been around a woman who brought out so many conflicting emotions in him. One minute he wanted to protect her, while the next, the urge to ravish road him hard.

He took the opportunity to look at her face while she was distracted. Jack had been right when he noted her girl-next-door appearance. There was nothing special about her individual features, but taken together the effect was...breathtaking.

Jack had dated some of the most beautiful women in the world. He'd had to in his past profession. It was all part of the playboy image he'd carefully cultivated. No one knew that he was originally a farm boy from a small town in the Missouri Ozarks. So why did he have a sudden urge to spill everything to this prickly flight attendant?

Maybe it was the fact that she didn't fawn over him like the others or expect him to lavish her with gifts on the first date. Was this a date? He glanced at the food on the table. It certainly qualified for one in his mind.

Jack was used to women wanting him for his money, but Delaney wouldn't follow suit. And that, more than anything, appealed to the man who walked off that farm seventeen years ago.

He stared at her in wonder for a few seconds before remembering himself. Delaney didn't know that he was loaded. He didn't make a habit of telling anyone. Would her behavior change once she found out? He didn't know and decided to delay that information for as long as possible.

She wasn't quick to give away her secrets. The element of mystery he found in her eyes, her smile and even her laughter drew him to her. That aloofness would make getting her into his bed a challenge, but the payoff would be far sweeter than anything he'd experienced in a very long time.

"How long have you been a flight attendant?" he asked.

"Not long." She met his gaze, brown eyes clashing with blue.

Jack felt the connection like a sucker punch to the gut. "That explains the tomato juice."

She frowned. "I apologize for that. It really was an accident."

"I know, but I can't say that I'm sorry it happened."

She cocked her head in confusion. "What do you mean?"

Jack brushed her fingertips with the back of his knuckles. The color in Delaney's face deepened to crimson and emotion swirled in her chocolate depths. He noted the spark of desire, along with something else that wasn't so easily identifiable. "If you hadn't spilled the juice, we might not be having dinner together right now."

He raised his glass of water. "Here's to happy accidents and new friendships."

DELANEY'S HAND quivered as she clinked her glass with Jack's. It wasn't an accident that they'd met. They could never be friends or anything else for that matter. The thought left her decidedly unsettled. She refused to look at the reasons too closely. Why had a man with double majors in art and law chosen to become an arms dealer? He could've done anything with his life. Instead, to her mind, he'd thrown it all away. Delaney's stomach soured at the loss.

"So what is it you do, Jack Gordon?" she asked.

He set his roast beef sandwich on the plate, his blue eyes piercing as they surveyed her face. Dishes clanked as someone cleared the table at the booth beside them. Delaney wondered if Jack would tell her the truth. For some reason that had nothing to do with the case, she hoped he did.

"I'm retired," he said finally, evading the question.

Delaney released a breath she hadn't realized she'd held.

"Lucky you. I wish I could retire so young," she said, ignoring the tinge of disappointment tightening her chest.

"I'm not *that* young." Jack actually blushed. The color gave his face a boyish cast, despite the hint of shadow covering his firm jaw.

"How old are you?" she asked, wiping her suddenly sweaty palms on her pants.

"Old enough."

Delaney shook her head. "Do you always evade direct questions?"

Jack grinned and winked at her. "Not always."

"Right." His playful words sobered Delaney, reminding her once again why she was here. Jack seemed like good company, but this was no ordinary dinner date. No matter how much she longed to fall into his blue depths and taste his firm lips, she couldn't. Delaney owed it to her sister to make sure that no one else's family had to suffer the way theirs had. If those weapons made it into the wrong hands, loss of life was guaranteed. Jack could prevent that from happening. Or at least she hoped that he could.

Delaney stared at him, giving herself time to take in his features. There was no denying the attraction she felt toward Jack. He made her want things she shouldn't want—like sex. She reminded herself again that he was an arms dealer…or used to be. No amount of charm and wishing could change that fact.

They finished their meal, flirting occasionally and making small talk. Jack was very good at both, while Delaney had to work at it. She was a little out of practice from taking the year off. He rose to help her out of the booth, allowing an elderly woman to pass by first.

"Ma'am," he said, giving the woman a slight nod, before turning his attention back to Delaney.

Did arms dealers respect their elders? It seemed out of character, but she could detect no ulterior motive.

"I'll give you one thing, you do have quite an appetite." There was no admonishment in Jack's voice when he spoke. He stared down at her empty plate in blatant admiration. "You must exercise like a fiend."

There was a time she'd been ashamed of her healthy appetite, going so far as to hide it, but no more. She refused to starve herself in order to impress a man. Not that it seemed to matter to Jack, since he looked genuinely pleased. "I do," Delaney admitted.

"You'd have to because there's not a gram of extra weight on your body." His voice dropped, then he added, "I checked."

Suddenly, the room seemed boiling hot. Delaney resisted the urge to tug at the blouse. For some reason, it never occurred to her that Jack would actually take the time to check her out. Sure, he'd flirted on the plane and given her his business card, but for all she knew, he handed them out like flyers on a street corner.

You are here as Delaney Carson, undercover agent, not Delaney Carter, the woman. Remember? The reminder did nothing to cool her body.

She dug her hand into her pocket and fished out some cash. "Here," she said, pushing the money toward him.

"I have it," he said, glancing at the bills clutched in her fingers as if he'd never seen money before.

"But this wasn't a date."

His eyes moved to her mouth. "It wasn't?"

A waitress walked by before she could answer, carrying a huge tray. Delaney stepped forward into Jack to avoid being hit. Their bodies brushed and her senses came alive. His subtle cologne surrounded her and she inhaled.

Jack's eyes flared and he glanced around the restaurant before taking a step back. "We'd—" he cleared his throat "—better get going."

He pressed his palm into her lower back and guided her outside after paying the bill. Delaney was proud that she managed to walk without wobbling. The touch was a simple act, not meant to evoke such a rush of sensation. Yet the heat of his fingers scalded her skin, making her nipples grow taut and heavy.

Delaney fought the urge to reach for his hand. They walked across the parking lot to her awaiting Chevy, then stopped at her door. She turned to face him.

The mild night held a hint of ocean air. Jack dropped his hand, only to brush a lock of her brown hair away from her face where a breeze had blown it. His fingertips were soft, caressing as he lingered over her skin.

"I'd really like to see you again," he said, the deep baritone of his voice lowering a half octave as he stared hard into her eyes.

Delaney's mouth went dry. Jack took a step closer, crowding her space. Their bodies didn't touch, but she felt the heat radiating from his flesh nonetheless. Her heart jumped in her chest. She knew in that instant that he was about to kiss her. Even more surprising was the fact that she really wanted him to. Delaney knew this could be part of the assignment going in, but that knowledge hadn't prepared her for the impact Jack's nearness would have on her.

She shuddered.

"Relax, I won't bite...unless you want me to." His hand trailed over the side of her neck, along the pulse jumping in her throat, and down her arm before settling on her hip. He didn't hold her tight, but his grip was firm, letting her know without words that he wasn't about to let her escape.

JACK PULLED HER CLOSER. He'd wanted to taste her since he'd first laid eyes on her, and now he was about to get his chance. His fingers flexed on her hip and she trembled.

Something primal rose inside of him. He inhaled, taking in the sweet odor of her skin. She didn't wear perfume like the women he'd previously dated. Delaney held a more subtle fragrance. Fresh and clean with a bit of citrus thrown in. He'd bet his boat that it was the soap she'd used.

Her lips pursed and her breathing accelerated. Jack's fingers quivered from the visceral punch. He lowered his head to her mouth, giving her plenty of time to pull away. Thank goodness she didn't. Jack wasn't sure if he would've survived the rebuff.

He skimmed her lips on first passing, a tease of things to come. The breath exploded out of his lungs as newfound urgency wrapped around his gut. He'd meant to draw out the tension and take it slow, but her soft, pliant mouth beckoned, while her taste intoxicated him. Jack groaned, giving in to temptation. He dove in, sealing their lips as his lids fell.

The kiss seared his mind, sending his blood supply south. Soft and warm, her feminine scent surrounded him, circling his head, leaving him dizzy with desire. When was the last time he experienced this sensation?

Jack frowned.

Had he *ever* felt like this? The answer left him shaken— and hungry for what Delaney could give him. Jack wanted to ravage her, take her right here in Jerry's parking lot. Onlookers be damned.

DELANEY'S WORLD SPUN. The taste of Jack nearly drowned her senses. He was like the finest scotch and the most primitive male all rolled into one. Her fingers pressed into his arms, sinking into his strength, before sliding around his neck. The hair at his nape brushed her knuckles in a satin caress and she moaned, taking a step closer until their bodies met.

His hands tightened, bunching in her shirt as he deepened the embrace. Jack's tongue slid along the seam of her mouth, probing, questing. Delaney opened and he plunged inside. She thought she was hot before, but she went molten as their tongues touched.

His mouth worked hers, drawing from her depths, while stoking her need. It was an expert game of give and take, while promising more to come. And oh, how she wanted more. Delaney's fingers raked his scalp as their bodies squirmed to get impossibly closer.

Heat and ripped muscle surrounded her as his hard sex nudged her belly. Delaney gasped and stepped back out of his embrace, when everything inside of her screamed for her to continue.

Her fingers instantly moved to her mouth as she tried to calm her raging hormones. "I—I'm sorry. Not sure what came over me. I don't normally allow men to kiss me so soon after meeting them."

"Me, neither," he said, laughing.

Delaney let out a nervous giggle.

Air sawed in and out of Jack's lungs as their laughter died. His eyes had gone from Newman blue to navy and his high cheekbones were slightly reddened. He didn't bother to hide his desire. "Will I see you again?" his voice cracked as he spoke.

"Yes," she said, breathlessly.

"When?" He shoved his hands into his pockets.

"I have to fly back to Phoenix tomorrow." Delaney knew Jack was scheduled on her flight.

He took a staggering breath. "I do, too. Will you be spending the night or continuing onto another destination?"

"I live there."

His face lit up. "What a coincidence. Maybe we could go out tomorrow night, if that's not too soon for you."

"No, I'd like that." Delaney pressed a button on her keys and moved to open the door. Their hands met as Jack reached the door handle before her. For a beat, Delaney didn't move. Her heart hammered repeatedly as their eyes locked. She forced herself to pull away.

Jack opened the door and waited for her to step in. He shut it behind her after she'd buckled her seat belt. Delaney started the vehicle, then hit a button to roll down the window.

"Until tomorrow night then." He stared, eating her alive with his eyes. She started the car and put it in gear.

"'Til then," she agreed.

Jack knocked on the roof as she drove off.

Delaney couldn't seem to stop shaking. She wanted to turn the car around and jump Jack's bones. Well, one bone in particular. Her body ached with need as she forced herself to drive to the Doubletree Guest Suites. Why now? Why Jack Gordon? Of all the people she could have been drawn to, why did it have to be a sexy gunrunner, a man she couldn't have?

She walked into the room as the phone rang. Delaney knew who it was before answering. "Carter," she said.

Roger McMillan's voice boomed on the other end of the line. "Where in the hell have you been? Why is your cell off? I've been calling for over an hour."

"Having dinner with Jack Gordon." That shut him up for a second. She wasn't about to mention the kiss. Strangely, it seemed far too personal to drag into the case.

"Excellent," he said finally, "because we have a problem. We've received intel from our street contacts that the shipment has been moved up by a day or so. The potential buyers that we know about are on the move. It's the unknown quantities that have us concerned."

Delaney plopped into the chair in front of the desk. "What do you mean it's been 'moved up'? We only had two weeks to begin with and half that time I've spent training to be a flight attendant."

"I'm sorry the criminals are screwing with your schedule, Agent Carter. Would you like me to phone them and ask for an extension?" Papers shuffled and she heard the scrawling of a pen in the background.

"No, sir."

"Well that's good, since I don't have them on speed dial. Did you get the file on David Rico?"

"Yes, I received it. What's our next move with him?"

"We don't have one. His name popped as a potential in, but since he's so low on the food chain we won't act unless absolutely necessary. Now where are we with Jack Gordon?"

Delaney ran a hand through her hair. "Not far. Despite the fact we had dinner, he's a hard man to pin down. He books multiple flights, so I've missed him once. I got lucky this last time." Her face heated as she remembered exactly how lucky she'd been.

"Do I need to remind you how important this is to the bureau? People's safety is at stake. Special-Agent-in-Charge Anderson is threatening to take over the investigation. Whatever Gordon did to him in the past, he hasn't forgotten it. He wants to take him down, along with the people behind the shipment. We're working on identifying the players, but with so many arms dealers in the country, it's like trying to play pin the tail on the donkey in the dark."

Delaney heard a noise in the background and knew he'd set down his coffee cup. She steeled herself, blocking out the pleasure she'd experienced moments ago. "I'm well aware of the importance of locating the shipment and stopping the weapons before they've been transported. I've made plans to meet with Gordon tomorrow night." Jack's face flashed in her mind and desire filled her once more.

"Do whatever it takes to get close to him."

Delaney pictured her and Jack, bodies intertwined. That wasn't what McMillan meant. Was it? Of course not. She shook her head to rid herself of the carnal image.

"We need to know about this shipment and if he's involved in any capacity."

"What if he isn't?" she asked, recalling the fact that Jack mentioned his retirement over dinner. He could be lying. She almost wished that he was, since it would make things so much easier, but Delaney didn't think so.

"Then Gordon will know who is and we'll use that information. Hopefully that will be enough to get Anderson off his back. The man's practically turned Gordon into his personal crusade."

"Have you uncovered any information about Gordon's past gun sales yet?"

"I've only managed to trace the past five years of his activities, but I'll keep trying."

She sighed. She had to know the truth. The sooner the better. Speculation only fueled her frustration.

"You don't have a problem with using Jack, do you?" McMillan asked. "If you do, I need to know now."

Guilt surged through her. Delaney couldn't seem to swallow past the lump clogging her throat. She knew if she said the wrong thing McMillan would yank her from the case. Her promotion was riding on her success, along with her career. Delaney refused to acknowledge the possibility that there was now more going on here than an assignment.

"No, sir." Her voice hitched. "I don't have a problem using him."

"Spoken like a true GS7 agent," he growled, slamming the phone down.

4

DELANEY WATCHED the sun creep over the hotel and pierce the ocean waves, turning the gray water to silver. Her eyes burned as she sipped the pungent coffee she'd made hours earlier. In a short time, she'd have to be at the airport and ready to board her flight.

The thought of facing one hundred and thirty-seven passengers with a smile affixed to her face made her want to hurl. This job could not be over soon enough. Too bad that wasn't what had kept her awake all night.

Jack Gordon's face flashed before her. Delaney had replayed their kiss in her mind repeatedly. She'd slowed it down, sped it up and even switched angles to catch the subtle nuances. No matter how she viewed the embrace, she'd been unable to diminish its impact.

Even now, she could still taste Jack on her lips. Brushing her teeth hadn't helped. Her mouth practically tingled in remembrance. She groaned in frustration and ran her fingers through her disheveled hair.

She stared at the shoreline, watching a few runners out for their early morning jog. If she weren't so exhausted, she'd join them. Her gaze scanned the beach, straining to see the shoreline to the south. Somewhere out there a cache of weapons waited for the bad guys to ship them. The questions were:

Who was behind the deal, how would they move them and where were they now?

If she knew those three answers, she wouldn't need to involve Jack Gordon at all.

Was it her fault that he'd put himself in this position? Had Jack decided against selling guns for a living, she wouldn't be having this conversation with herself. She also would not have spent half the night dreaming about him, reliving the kiss, imagining what it would feel like to have his muscled body moving on top of hers. Instead, she would've experienced the real thing.

That last image had woken her from a sound sleep and left her aching. Delaney hadn't slept since. She glanced at the clock. Six blinked back. She sighed. Soon it would be time to throw on her imaginary cape and become "Super Stew."

JACK TURNED OVER and punched his pillow. He was hard again. Not an unusual phenomena in the morning, but he'd been like this all night—ever since he'd kissed Delaney Carson. It had been a long time since he wanted a woman this bad. In fact, Jack couldn't recall *ever* craving a woman like this.

Twice he'd woken and had to take matters into his own hands. That alone had shocked him, since it would've been easy enough to make a phone call and have someone join him for the night. Trouble was, he didn't want just anyone in his bed. He wanted Delaney Carson.

He chose not to look too closely at why. He had a feeling he wasn't ready to face that answer just yet. Jack glanced down his body. There was no mistaking his need. He threw the sheets back and padded naked to the bathroom adjacent to the master suite. He turned all the body jets on to full cold, then stepped under the spray, hoping the water beat his erection into submission.

The temperature took his breath away and eventually had the desired effect on his body. Jack shut the shower off and grabbed a nearby towel from the heated rack. He watched the news on the screen behind his bathroom mirror as he shaved.

"Homeland Security raised their threat level today. According to sources, an unidentified group are attempting to smuggle in weapons and the items necessary to build a dirty bomb," the news anchor said, before adding, "attempts to confirm this information are inconclusive."

Jack snorted. "Big surprise there." For a moment, he considered checking with a few old sources to find out if the threat was real. In the end, Jack decided against that brash move. He was out of the business and he planned to stay out.

He hit a button and the screen dimmed. The car he'd hired to take him to the airport should be here within an hour. Jack's chest tightened at the thought of seeing Delaney tonight. He could still taste her sweetness on his lips. It was as tantalizing as the woman herself.

Jack glanced down at the front of the tented towel wrapped around his waist and cursed. If he didn't get his body under control soon, by the time he got her naked he'd embarrass himself.

"Enough already," he said, hoping this time his body listened.

DAVID RICO SAT behind his desk in an Aeron chair, tapping on the keyboard until the numbers he sought appeared on his flat-screen computer monitor. Those seven digits brought a smile to his face as he sat back and peered out the window at the dazzling Pacific Ocean.

In a few days, he would be a very rich man, permanently establishing himself in the world of arms trafficking. The weapons would arrive in Long Beach tomorrow via tanker. It would take a couple of days to ensure the merchandise hadn't been detected. Once he'd done that, it was only a matter of getting the items out of the city so he could auction them off.

So far, everything had gone off without a hitch. Well, almost everything. David frowned at the reminder. It was time to address his transportation problem. He hit a button on his desk.

"Tony?"

"Yes, Mr. Rico."

"Could you please show Mr. Sullivan in?"

"Yes, sir. Right away."

David hit another button, this one tucked discreetly under his desktop, and the door to his oceanfront office opened with a soft click.

"Right this way, Mr. Sullivan," Tony said, stepping aside for the man to enter. Tony's dark gaze shot over Sullivan's head to meet Rico's.

Fred Sullivan ambled in wearing a tweed suit to cover his forty-five-year-old body, which washed out his olive coloring and left him with a jaundiced appearance. His black hair and moustache tilted at a peculiar angle, aided by a healthy dollop of gel.

David glanced at the man with disgust, then gave an almost imperceptible nod to Tony, who then locked the door and flicked a switch that lowered the blinds over the floor-to-ceiling bulletproof windows.

Fred Sullivan's startled look darted to Tony, then back to Rico. David smiled invitingly, feeling anything but.

"The light irritated my eyes," he lied. "Please take a seat, Mr. Sullivan." David indicated the chair across from his desk.

Fred wiped his trembling hands on his trousers, stepped forward and sat.

"Can I get you anything, Mr. Sullivan?" Rico asked.

He shook his head.

"Very well, let's get down to it."

"Mr. Rico, thank you again for taking time out of your busy schedule to see me," began Fred.

David smiled again, feeling the cold thrill of Sullivan's fear wash over him. "I always have time to meet with a colleague."

Fred relaxed visibly and used his sleeve to mop his sweaty brow. "We have a problem moving the shipment out of L.A."

David cocked his head and furrowed his brow. "I'm sorry. I must have misunderstood you. Did you say we?"

"Yes, sir. I mean, *I* have a problem," he added hastily.

Rico sat forward, resting his hands on his desk. "And what would that be?" he asked, knowing full well that Sullivan had failed to get the trucks that would ferry the weapons.

Fred squirmed like a bug pinned to a dissecting lab table, then shot a glance over his shoulder at Tony, who hadn't moved. "They were supposed to be here by now, but there's been a holdup and it looks like they won't arrive until next week," Fred said, fingering the cuff of his suit jacket.

David sat back, pretending to consider Sullivan's words. The trucks in question had been specifically designed to safely transport the weapons. They came with false interiors and padded shelving that couldn't be replaced by stealing any old semi-truck. Nor could they afford a one-week delay with the feds beginning to poke their heads in where they did not belong. The buyers wouldn't wait forever. There was no time to re-schedule the auction.

Anger rolled through Rico, searing his insides, while on the outside he appeared as calm as ever. Tony's eyes widened and he took a step back, a clear indication that he knew the truth.

At five foot seven and one hundred-thirty pounds, David Rico knew he wasn't physically imposing. What he lacked in strength and size, he more than made up for in imagination. "What do you propose we do about this problem, Mr. Sullivan?"

"I—I told you. We should put the transport off until next week."

David shook his head admonishingly. "Now you and I

both know that's not possible. We're dealing with very busy people. People who'll think nothing of taking their business elsewhere, if I go back on my word."

"B-but the trucks won't arrive in time."

"Then I guess I'll just have to come up with some other way of getting the merchandise out of town." He already had a backup plan in place, but would only use it in the event of an emergency. The plan would require paying off too many people, which would significantly cut in to his profits. No, he definitely wouldn't use it until he'd exhausted all other avenues.

Fred smiled. "Good idea, sir."

"Why thank you, Mr. Sullivan. That's kind of you to say." David tapped the keyboard, clearing his computer screen and ignoring the man sitting in front of him.

Fred Sullivan's smile slowly faded. "Mr. Rico, sir. I'm sorry to disturb you again, but what would you like me to do?"

"Do?" Rico questioned. "Why nothing, Mr. Sullivan. Our business arrangement concluded with your failure to deliver."

"B-but you said we'd have to come up with some other way to move the goods."

David shook his head. "No, I said *I* would. Tony, please escort Mr. Sullivan out the back way."

Tony nodded, then opened a door that up until then had blended seamlessly with the wall.

Sullivan walked toward Rico's able-bodied assistant.

"Hold up," David called, raising his hand to stop their progress.

Sullivan's smarmy face lit with hope.

"On second thought, Tony, why don't you take Mr. Sullivan fishing off Catalina Island. I hear the great white are biting this time of year."

Fred paled and started to move away.

"Yes, sir," Tony said, latching on to the man.

Rico met Fred's hazel eyes. The man screamed.

"Now, now, there is no cause for hysterics. Remember, the room is soundproof. If you can't conduct yourself like a gentleman, I'm going to have to ask Tony to assist you. It was nice doing business with you, Mr. Sullivan. Enjoy the boat ride. The water should be positively refreshing."

David picked up the phone to dial Hirosuke as Tony closed the door behind them. All this talk about fish had put him in the mood for sushi.

***

THE BOARDING AREA was packed to the gills with passengers. Delaney groaned inwardly as she scanned the people. The flight looked like it was going to be pre-board hell. She didn't see Jack Gordon, which was probably for the best. She was in no mood to put up with his cheerful banter and easy charm. Delaney's hands shook from the caffeine infusion she'd given herself earlier as she punched in the code to the jetway and swiped her ID badge.

The light blinked red.

What the—

She glared at the keypad and tried again.

The red light continued to blink.

Give me a break. Delaney jerked on the door.

"Having trouble?" Jeremy called out from behind her.

She turned to see him walk forward with his bag in tow.

"You look like the cat drug you in backward through a barbwire fence."

"I thought you said you weren't from Texas." Delaney glared at him, taking in his perfectly pressed uniform, freshly scrubbed face and manicured nails. In that moment, she debated whether to kick his starched ass.

Jeremy must have read her thoughts because he took a step back. "I'm not."

"Well, you sure sound like it when you say sh— Crap like that." Her gaze wandered to the passengers nearby who seemed a little too interested in their conversation for her peace of mind.

Jeremy snickered. "I see someone needs a nap."

"Don't start with me. Just open the door."

He strolled forward and stopped at the keypad. "What are the magic words?" he asked as he pressed the code into the alarm.

"I'll let you live if you open the door," she muttered between clenched teeth.

Jeremy started to say something, then stopped as if he'd thought better of it.

The door beeped and the light turned green. He glanced over his shoulder and arched a brow at Delaney before proceeding down the jetway, mumbling under his breath about moody women.

They'd barely managed to stow their luggage when the operations agent, or ops agent in airline lingo, hit the call button to signal he was about to board the aircraft. Delaney made her way forward.

The captain stepped out the cockpit as she reached the galley. "Are you guys overnighting with us in Kentucky?"

"I don't know about them, but I'm getting off in Phoenix." She didn't add that she planned to take a nap until her *date* with Jack Gordon this evening. She refused to give Jeremy the satisfaction of knowing that he'd been right about her appearance.

"Too bad," he said, giving her a quick once-over. "I was hoping you could join me for dinner. Maybe when I get back to base in a couple of days we could go for a drive in my Porsche."

Delaney tried to seem interested, the least she could do was try for polite. "Thanks, but I'll pass," she said, in no mood to complicate an already complicated situation. Jack was more than enough for her to handle at the moment.

People continued to board, carrying their lives in their luggage. It would be a full boat today. Their faces became an endless blur until she spotted the end of the line. Delaney greeted the last individual and prepared to shut the door, ignoring her disappointment that Jack hadn't made it aboard. *Stop being silly. He'll catch another flight. You'll see him soon enough,* the voice in her head chastised.

Fingers shot out, catching the forward entry door before she could close it. Talk about cutting it close.

Delaney swung the door wide, then opened her mouth to welcome the straggler.

Jack Gordon greeted her with a bright smile. "I almost *missed* you," he said, inflecting a very different meaning to the statement.

Delaney's heart thumped as she watched him walk down the aisle. Today he didn't wear a jacket. There was nothing obscuring her view of his tight butt and long, long legs. She drank in the view of his wide shoulders and slim hips as Jack waited for the person on the aisle to rise so he could reach his window seat.

"Are you going to shut the door so we can push back?" the ops agent asked, jolting her out of her ogling.

She did the only thing she could think of to hide her embarrassment. Delaney slammed the front entry door and armed the slides. Then she reached for the microphone at the front of the cabin.

"Flight attendants, prepare doors."

"Cross check," Barbie drawled in reply.

Delaney put the mic down and walked to the cockpit door. "The cabin is secured," she said before shutting it.

Jeremy made his way up the aisle. He grabbed the demo equipment and stood facing the cabin. "Do you want to talk or walk this time?"

"I'll walk," Delaney said, reaching for the seat belt demo. Maybe if she moved, the blood in her body would stop pooling in places that made her throb.

Jeremy grasped the mic. "To properly fasten your seat belts slide that flat head into the buckle. To unfasten, lift up on the flip latch and it'll release. Seat belts should be worn tight and low across those oh, so slender hips."

Delaney demonstrated and tried not to laugh.

"There may be fifty ways to leave your lover, but there are only eight ways to leave this aircraft. Two forward entry doors, four overwing window exits and two aft entry doors...that's in the back for those of you sitting in the tail section."

Delaney held up her fingers and pointed to each exit. She felt like an idiot. No wonder people made fun of this part of the demonstration. She looked as if she were directing a symphony that only held eight notes.

Not meaning to, her gaze strayed to Jack, locking onto his handsome face. Heat scrolled down her body as he gave her a leisurely visual caress. Delaney shifted under his regard, trying to ignore her body's reaction. He followed her movements with such raw yearning that she felt the pull all the way to her bones.

Delaney tore her attention away. Jeremy was still talking. It took her a second to realize that she should've been walking down the aisle at this stage of the announcements. Delaney flushed and hurried, pressing one hand to each bin to ensure they were locked as she checked the luggage at the feet of each passenger.

"You need to push that under the seat for takeoff and landing," she said, making her way to the rear of the airplane. She knew the second she was out of Jack's line of sight. The heat instantly left her body and damned if she didn't miss it.

Delaney made her way forward. She barely glanced at

Jack as she walked to her jumpseat. His gaze was back on her. She could feel it between her shoulder blades, melting through her uniform, leaving a puddle in its wake.

She sat, buckling in, before quickly crossing her arms over her chest to hide her body's reaction. She obviously wasn't fast enough. Delaney glanced in time to see Jack's lips tilt and his eyes smolder like embers in a fire.

Her face flared even hotter, so she picked up a briefing card to fan herself. Jack knew exactly what he was doing to her.

Jeremy leaned in next to her ear. "Honey, if the sexual tension in here gets any thicker between you two," he said, indicating Jack, "the electricity will fry us all."

"There's nothing going on between us."

"Humph, yeah, sure, and Barbara and I are getting married next week."

Delaney broke away from Jack's gaze with effort to look at the attendant beside her. "Not now, Jeremy."

He turned his shoulder to her. "I stand by my earlier statement."

She sighed. "Which was?"

"Someone needs a nap."

5

DELANEY WAS GRATEFUL that with the exception of Jack's constant attention, the flight remained blissfully uneventful. The aircraft pulled in to the gate and she opened the door.

"Bah-bye, bye, bye, bu-bye." She grinned as the passengers disembarked. This was her favorite part of the flight because she got to leave the plane. She wondered how many flight attendants felt the same way.

Jack waited in his seat until most of the aircraft had emptied before walking up the aisle. A smile played on his lips as he approached. Delaney handed him a slip of paper with her number scrawled on it.

"See you tonight," he said, a wealth of promise ringing in the simple phrase.

Delaney considered canceling as she was hit with a sudden flurry of nerves, but she knew she wouldn't. The deadline for the shipment loomed over her. It didn't matter that her body craved Jack's touch or that Delaney could still feel the scorch of his lips. She'd find someone else to fill the need he'd so easily created inside of her once this assignment ended.

Delaney pulled her bag through the airport, staring at the barren mountains that surrounded Phoenix. Some people hated the Valley of the Sun, as it was affectionately called by the locals, because they thought the desert was devoid of life.

Delaney knew better. This place teamed with life and she loved every craggy inch of it.

She drove home, staring at Camelback Mountain in the distance. The odd-shaped rock got its name for the sleeping camel outline you could see at certain angles. Delaney enjoyed climbing the mountain in the winter months.

Delaney pulled into the drive of her modest concrete cinderblock home. The lemon tree's branches in the front yard dipped low under the weight of ripening fruit. She'd been meaning to pick the lemons, but had never gotten around to it. Delaney hit a button on her visor and her garage door opened with a loud screech.

She cringed, glancing at the neighbors' houses to make sure no one had come out to investigate the sound. The garage was one more item on her to-do list that had fallen by the wayside while she worked toward her master's.

"I'm home," she called out to the vast emptiness, closing the connecting garage door behind her.

The air in the house smelled of neglect. A plastic plant Delaney had purchased to imbue life to the kitchen lay covered in a thick film of dust. She ignored the sudden twinge of guilt and glanced into the living room. A mountain of mail rose from the hardwood floor, climbing toward the slot in her front door. Delaney scooped up the letters and took them into her office.

Had a tornado touched down while she was out of town?

She placed the envelopes onto what she hoped was her desk and headed down the short pictureless hall to her bedroom. The white comforter called out her name. Delaney walked the few feet separating her from paradise and fell face-first onto the bed.

Dreams of Jack started the second Delaney's head hit the pillow. They were no longer standing in Jerry's Deli parking lot kissing. Instead, they'd moved to the privacy of a billowy tent on the beach that housed only one item, a massive bed. One second she was dressed. The next, her clothing lay in a pile at her feet and Jack proceeded to pleasure her with his hands and his mouth.

DELANEY WOKE TO the sound of the phone ringing. The room was dark and she had yet to recover from the dream. What was the time? Where was she? For that matter, where was Jack? It took her a few seconds to recall that she was at home and supposed to meet Jack for a date. As much as she wanted to solve this case, Delaney wasn't sure she could go through with it. Jack's kiss obviously had left her more shaken than she'd first thought.

The phone rang again and she reached for the receiver. Her hand hovered above the cordless for a moment, before drawing back. The last chirping sound died in the air, leaving deafening silence behind. She'd agreed to go out to dinner with him. She couldn't back out now. Delaney took a deep breath. Jack probably thought she was standing him up. What had she done?

She couldn't blow off Jack because she was worried about what might happen. It was only a dream for heaven's sake. McMillan was counting on her. She was quite capable of ignoring Jack's advances…if she wanted to. Delaney straightened. She'd have to be strong, for the sake of the mission and her sanity. She hoped she wasn't too late.

Delaney sprinted through the house, flipping on lights as she searched for her purse. She'd shoved Jack's card inside. She was probably the last person on the planet without caller ID or an answering machine. At first, Delaney hadn't wanted those items, since her cell was equipped with both options. Later, school had taken over and she didn't have time to get them installed.

"Please, please, please," she said, dumping the contents onto her counter. The business card plopped out last with a breath mint stuck to the back of it.

Her hands shook as she dialed the number. Jack answered on the third ring. "Hello?"

"It's Delaney."

"I thought maybe you'd forgotten about tonight," he said relief in his voice

"No, I was in the shower," she lied.

"I forgot to ask where you live."

Delaney glanced around her house at the neglect. "Why don't we meet somewhere? Pick a spot."

"I take it you live somewhere central."

"Yeah, I do, so as long as you don't pick Apache Junction, I can be anywhere within forty minutes." She padded the number to give herself enough time to shower and change. She couldn't exactly arrive for dinner in her uniform.

"Is fusion okay?"

"Sounds great."

"Why don't we meet at Sanctuary on Camelback Road in say, forty-five minutes?"

"I'll be there," she said, too cheerily. Delaney hung up the phone and heaved a sigh of relief. That was close, too close. She didn't want to think about what McMillan would've done to her if she'd stood Jack up on a date. What was she saying? This wasn't a date. If she'd missed a rendezvous with her target, she corrected herself. The situation didn't bear thinking about.

Despite Delaney's resolve to hurry, she found herself lingering in the shower and taking her time to apply a light coat of makeup. Something she rarely, if ever, did. She dried her hair, styling it with some mousse until it fell around her face in soft waves. She glanced once more in the mirror, twirled, then watched the bell of her dark trouser legs fall modestly to her ankles. She tugged at the sleeves of her cream colored blouse.

She took a reassuring breath, then let it out slowly. Her heart hammered in her chest as she placed the items she'd need into her purse if they ended up back at Jack's place for a nightcap. Delaney reached into her bedside table and grabbed her computer key drive, staring for several seconds at the box of condoms she kept there. Since there would be no sex, she wouldn't need those, she thought, before grabbing three and shutting the drawer.

Delaney raced to Camelback Road. It was easy enough to find Sanctuary, even though she'd never been there. She parked her car and walked toward the restaurant. Jack stood inside the door, waiting.

Dressed in casual chic, Jack didn't so much wear clothes, as allow them to drape his form. It was an ability not many people outside of the modeling world possessed, but he did.

"Glad to see you again. You look fabulous. The outfit suits you. Soft as silk." He fingered the collar of her pale shirt. "Yet, no nonsense," he said, glancing at her navy pants, before leaning in to kiss the side of her head. His unique cologne surrounded her, dampening the aroma of the spices filling the air. Delaney fought to keep from turning into the kiss. Her stomach rumbled, but it wasn't for food.

"Hungry?" he asked, his gaze searching.

"Famished." Delaney licked her lips.

His eyes clouded with desire as he followed the movement of her tongue. "Do you still want to eat here?"

She watched the column of his throat work up and down as he swallowed hard. She longed to trace the length with her tongue, taste the salt of his skin. "Where else could we go?"

His eyes flashed in speculation. "I could fix us something back at my place."

"You cook?"

He grinned. "Among other things."

"How could I possibly refuse an offer like that?" The truth was she couldn't. Delaney needed to get inside Jack's home. She'd search the place, copy the files off his computer, do recon in hopes of finding the info she sought without having to come right out and ask. She doubted under the circumstances that Jack would be very cooperative.

That was the only reason she had allowed him to change their dinner plans, or so she told herself. So why didn't she believe it?

"Let's grab a drink before we go," he suggested.

"That would be lovely. I've never been here before, but I have heard great things about the restaurant."

Jack guided Delaney to the bar. "What would you like?"

"Anything but tequila. I had a bad experience with that drink back in college and I've never recovered."

"Where did you go to school?"

"Boston."

He smiled. "Is your family there?"

Delaney's cheer sagged a second, then she quickly recovered. "Yes, what about you?"

"Columbia, Missouri." He laughed. "I think, no matter where you went to school, everyone has had at least one similar experience. Mine wasn't tequila. Let's just say that bourbon is not my friend."

"Kindred spirits," she said, realizing that she actually meant it. She and Jack may be on opposite sides, but their personalities were similar. They appeared to enjoy many of the same things, but it was hard to tell what was real and what wasn't. The rules of the game were changing faster than Delaney could keep up.

She tried to ignore the warmth coming from Jack's palm and

the tingle it sent up her spine. His fingers barely brushed her, yet Delaney felt the effects of the touch all the way to her earlobes.

He found them a couple of bar stools and waited for her to take her seat, before he joined her. The bartender handed him a menu and Jack began to scan the list. "Two glasses of the ninety-eight Sancerre."

The drinks arrived a few moments later and Jack raised his glass. "To new beginnings."

"May they last," Delaney said, wishing she could mean it. "So, how long have you lived in Phoenix?"

"Not long, but I like it so far. And you?"

Delaney tilted her head to stare into his face. "Long enough to get used to the heat...if that's ever possible."

He took a sip of wine. "Yes, I've been told that it takes a while to acclimate."

"Some people never do."

His gaze locked onto her face. "I don't know. Certain kinds of heat can be quite enjoyable."

Delaney's brow rose. "I guess it depends on what's causing it."

Jack's lips twitched. "I can think of a few ways worth exploring."

"Are you flirting with me again, Mr. Gordon?"

"I believe I am, Ms. Carson. Do you have a problem with that?" he asked in challenge.

Delaney grinned. "Only if you stop."

Jack laughed. "Not a chance."

That's what she was afraid of. Delaney squirmed on the bar stool, attempting to get comfortable. It was impossible, sitting so close to him. It felt like every hair on her body had turned into an antenna and they were all pointed at Jack.

She needed to move, to walk, to run far, far away. Instead, Delaney glanced into his face, allowing herself to linger on his long lashes, the deep blue of his eyes and that electric grin that sent shockwaves through her.

"What brings you to the Valley?" she asked.

Jack shrugged. "Some things just get old after a while. I've lived in Malibu for over ten years. I like it well enough, but wouldn't want to try to raise a family there."

Delaney blinked. She couldn't help it. That was the absolute last thing she'd expected Jack to say. In all her years of dating, she'd never once heard a man talk about settling down.

"I see from your stunned expression that I've surprised you." Jack ran his finger around the mouth of his wineglass.

"No. I mean. Yes. Maybe a little."

"Don't you ever think about hanging up your wings and finding somewhere to put down some roots?"

His rapt interest had Delaney fidgeting again. She hadn't really ever thought about roots. She'd been so focused on her job and trying to overcompensate for her sister's accident that she hadn't had time to consider the possibility that one day she'd meet someone that she'd want to commit to. At least not in any serious fashion. Delaney had never come across a guy who'd kept her attention long enough.

Until now, the insidious thought burrowed beneath her skin and straight into her heart.

"I suppose I haven't met the right guy yet—not that I'm looking," she added hastily. A rush of heat filled her face. "I have goals. Things I'd like to accomplish before that can happen."

"I've learned that there are some things that you just can't plan for." His expression was unreadable as the words left his mouth, but Delaney felt the deeper implication.

"Let's get out of here," she suggested out of sheer desperation. The last thing she needed was to get emotionally entangled in this assignment—it would lead to nothing but utter destruction.

Too late, the voice in her mind whispered again.

Delaney stood, refusing to give the voice credence. There was no way she would ever fall for an arms dealer, ex or otherwise. There were plenty of smart, charming, funny, good-looking single men left on this planet besides Jack Gordon. And she planned to find one, right after she closed this case and finished her master's degree.

She glanced at his face and automatically focused on his lips. The urge to kiss him was strong. Delaney fought it—hard.

Jack didn't wait for her to say another word. He threw money onto the bar, then slipped his hand in hers and tugged Delaney out the door and across the parking lot.

"Do you want to follow me or would you prefer that I drive?" Heat poured off his body, washing over her as he stepped closer.

"I prefer to be in control." Why had she said that? It was the truth, but she hadn't meant for it to sound so suggestive or like such a challenge. Delaney paused. She never lost control in a relationship. What was she saying? This wasn't a relationship and never would be.

"Control? Interesting choice of words." He looked at her knowingly. "Now why does that not surprise me?"

Again he didn't wait for an answer, but simply walked to his vehicle.

"Get in," he said, unlocking the car and opening the door for her.

She complied. Delaney knew this was her chance to get access to his Paradise Valley home. She ignored the voice reminding her that wasn't the reason she wanted to leave with Jack Gordon.

*By any means necessary...*McMillan's words filtered through her mind.

She fastened her seat belt as Jack drove across the parking

lot and stopped. "Is there a problem?" she asked, hoping he didn't hear the disappointment in her voice.

"You said you liked to be in control." He nodded to something outside the window.

Delaney glanced to her right and realized he'd stopped in front of her car. She laughed.

Jack grinned. "I don't have a problem with a woman who likes to keep on top of things. Sometimes giving up control can be fun."

"I wouldn't know."

"You should try it sometime." *Like tonight* was left unsaid. "You might enjoy it."

She opened the door and stepped out, before he could come around the car to do it for her.

"I'll drive slow," he called after her as she strolled to her car.

"Don't do it for my sake," she called to him, relishing the banter, even though she knew she was flirting with danger.

"I'll take that as a challenge." He hit a button and his tinted window closed with a soft hiss.

Delaney couldn't believe the words coming out of her mouth. It was as if another woman possessed her. One who knew just what to say, how to act, what to do. She was spending way too much time around Barbie and Jeremy. They were rubbing off. She refused to consider that it might be Jack who brought out her wanton side.

She'd rather believe she was simply playing the part of an experienced undercover agent, but Delaney knew there was more going on between her and Jack Gordon.

She followed him west through Paradise Valley. He didn't speed, but he hadn't slowed down for her, either. Delaney smiled to herself. Jack was a man of his word. That thought bothered her more than it should. So far she hadn't been able to catch him in a single lie. Everything he'd told her about where he went to school had been correct, according to his file. He'd been evasive about his profession, but he hadn't out-and-out lied.

Was he telling the truth about being retired?

Their cars continued to wind through the area. She should've known he'd live on the other side of Camelback Mountain. How many times had she hiked past his home? His drive twisted, snaking back and forth until they reached a contemporary house that blended in with the sand-colored boulders surrounding it.

Delaney parked in the circular drive and stepped out of her car. Lights from Phoenix and Paradise Valley blanketed the desert floor sparkling like fireflies in the darkness. The warm dry air brought the fragrance of wildflowers to her nose. Somewhere nearby Delaney heard the tinkling sounds of water as it spilled out of a fountain.

Jack pulled in to a garage and came out the front door a moment later.

"Great view," she said, crossing her arms over her chest. Could she really do this?

"Delaney, if you're not comfortable being here, we can go somewhere else for dinner. I don't mind."

She turned away from the city view to look at him. "You really don't mind, do you?" Most men would not be pleased, but as far as she could tell, Jack wasn't like most men.

The corners of his mouth kicked up. "I'll admit that I'd be a little disappointed, but mind…? No. I want you to be comfortable. We don't have to do anything you don't want to do."

The problem was she wanted to do everything with this man. Delaney glanced into his eyes. There was no guile in his blue depths, only truth. A wave of guilt swept through her as she thought about Elaine and how she'd never get to feel these sorts of things. Delaney told herself to make her excuses and leave. Break away before someone got the wrong idea... *like her.*

"Are you okay?" He took a step forward and grasped her elbow as if he thought she would collapse or run away.

She tried to smile, but her lips refused to cooperate. This assignment was starting to leave a bitter taste in her mouth. "I'm fine. Just light-headed from the lack of food," she lied smoothly.

"Let's get you inside, so I can whip something together for dinner. The only thing I want making you light-headed is me."

6

WHO KNEW JACK would turn out to be a pretty terrific cook? She'd been impressed while he skillfully chopped and diced vegetables and carried on a good conversation. Delaney was beginning to think he was a man of many talents.

She watched him covertly, while sipping her Merlot. His movements were fluid like water, not a waste of energy expelled. It captivated her. Jack held a grace she'd never possess. Which is why it surprised her, when he flipped a red pepper into the air and caught it with his mouth.

"You seem to have a flair for cooking," she said. "All your movements are so precise."

Jack ducked his head. "My mom insisted that all her sons know how to cook, dance and do laundry. And not necessarily in that order. She signed my brothers and I up for dance class by the time we were five. We took a lot of ribbing, but the girls seemed to like it. Mom let me quit dance class when I hit high school and made the varsity baseball team." He shrugged. "I guess some of the moves stuck with me."

Delaney's heart melted a little, despite her resolve to stay cold.

He tossed another pepper into the air and caught it.

"Do you want to give it a try?" he asked, a mischievous glint in his eyes.

"I probably shouldn't."

"Oh, come on," he urged. "Worried you won't be able to catch one?"

"No."

Delany giggled as the third piece of chopped pepper Jack had tossed landed on the floor. She tried to recall the last time she'd relaxed in the company of a man long enough to play. No one came to mind. How had Jack managed to bring out that hidden side of her so effortlessly?

"I tried to warn you," she said, attempting to catch another pepper. Who knew a date could be this fun? *Try never.* It's not a date. It's not a date. It's not a date. She hated having to remind herself.

"Are you even trying?" Jack asked, lobbing the pepper higher into the air.

The extra lift gave Delaney enough time to get under it. The tiny morsel dropped into her mouth in a taste explosion and she raised her arms in victory.

Jack clapped and they resumed a comfortable silence while he continued to cook.

The house seemed big from the outside, but now that she was inside, Delaney noted that it was enormous. Yet, the rooms exuded cozy warmth that belied their size. Everything was neat and in its proper place. He'd taken great care with the details, something she'd never managed to do. This was not only a house, this was a home.

A home that could pass for a museum, and considering the art she'd caught glimpses of when they'd first walked inside, Jack could open his home and charge admission.

Dealing arms paid very well indeed. Cold quickly enveloped her as she stared around the room at the priceless objects of art. How many lives had this collection cost?

"Is the wine all right?"

Delaney jumped at his question, interrupting her thoughts. "Yes, why do you ask?"

He grinned. "Because you aren't drinking it and you're scowling."

"Sorry." She grimaced. "Honestly, it's wonderful. Just like the dinner you're preparing. Thank you, again."

"You're welcome," he said, wiping his hands on a dish towel before slipping onto a bar stool beside her. Jack reached for his own glass of wine and took a sip. "Not bad if I do say so myself."

"You have a lovely home," Jack smiled. "Tell me more about yourself. What did you do before you became a flight attendant?" He raised the glass to his lips and took another drink.

"I worked in an office, gathering intel on…other companies."

Something sparked in his eyes at her words. "Sounds exciting."

"Sometimes it was, but most of the time it was fairly mundane. Definitely not what I expected, when I joined…was hired, I mean."

"Is that why you left?" he asked casually.

"They didn't give me much choice. It was either do the job they asked or get out." Delaney fingered the crystal stem of the glass. It wasn't too far from the truth. They hadn't asked her to do the job or leave. Instead, McMillan held her promotion above a chasm, threatening to drop it.

"That explains your uncertainty on the airplane."

"Flying takes some getting used to."

Jack rested his elbow on the breakfast bar. "Then why do it?"

Delaney shrugged. "To prove to everyone that I'm not afraid. And that I'm able to get the job done."

He placed his glass on the countertop. "I understand, but why pick flying? There must be other ways that you can prove yourself." *Safer* ways was left unspoken, but she heard it all the same.

Delaney opened her mouth to respond, but was distracted by Jack's collarbone. Something about the way the V of his shirt dipped, exposing tanned flesh and a hint of shadow had her longing to explore. She followed the line up to his jawline and onto his lips as he licked away a stray bead of wine. Her breath rushed from her lungs.

Positively lethal.

Heat infused Delaney, sending desire coursing through her body, leaving a trail of moisture behind. She tore her gaze away from his mouth and forced herself to focus.

"I'm sorry. What was the question?"

Amusement lit his face. "I asked you to tell me about yourself."

Delaney blinked. Caught ogling again. "Oh, me. I'm boring," She insisted. "I'd rather hear about you."

"You don't seem boring to me. In fact, you're a bit of a mystery. It's like I've been given pieces of Delaney Carson, but I can't quite see the picture." He sat back and studied her for several seconds. "Have I mentioned that I love to solve puzzles?"

She shook her head. This was one puzzle Jack wouldn't crack. "I work a lot. I don't really have time to do much else."

"I always thought flight attendants led such..." He waved his hand into the air as he searched for the right words. "High-flying lives."

Delaney thought about her typical Friday nights and nearly choked on her wine. She wondered what Jack would think about her idea of excitement. Would he be turned off by the fact that she grabbed take-out, then went home and lay on the couch in her sweats, watching old movies? Jack didn't seem like a movie-and-sweats kind of guy, she thought, glancing around his custom-designed kitchen.

"Define *exciting*," she said.

"You know." He lifted his glass to his mouth once more. "Different city every night. A guy in every port. Coffee, tea or me?"

"Yeah, it's that exciting all the time." Delaney snorted, causing her eyes to water as her wine nearly shot out of her nose. "You've been watching too many old 'made for television' movies about the golden age of flying."

Undeterred, Jack cocked his head. "Do you have men in every city?" He made the question sound casual, although Delaney got the distinct impression it was anything but.

"Not hardly. I haven't dated anyone seriously in years. Who has time with the schedule that I keep?" She almost told him how hard it was to date while working and going to school at the same time, but she stopped herself short. The comfort she felt with this man made it far too easy to slip and tell the truth. Delaney had to be more vigilant.

She tried to recall what her reasons were again, as the fragrance of his cologne mixed with warm man filled her senses.

"I find that hard to believe. A beautiful woman such as yourself, dateless? No way."

She sighed. "It's the truth, and for the record I'm not beautiful."

Elaine was the beautiful one. She'd proven that fact time and again by being crowned queen of various social events around Boston, while Delaney waited in the wings to blossom. In the end, she'd grown in her own way, but never managed to bloom. It had been a disappointment to her family that she hadn't followed in her sister's footsteps, but they'd recovered.

Delaney knew her parents loved her. They just had very traditional beliefs when it came to the roles of women in the workplace.

The only time Delaney thought about these things was when someone mentioned beauty, as Jack just had, which fortunately didn't occur often. Normally, it didn't bother her, but tonight was different.

Jack opened his mouth to protest, but she held up her hand to still his words.

"I'm not saying I go around scaring dogs and small children with my appearance. I know how to make the best of what I've been given. All I'm saying is that they aren't going to ask me to enter a beauty contest anytime soon. And no, I'm not fishing for a compliment."

"I know it's rude to disagree with a lady, but let's agree to disagree on the matter. Okay?" He glanced out at the city lights through the floor-to-ceiling windows that made up one wall of the kitchen.

"Do you see your family often?" she asked, deciding it was best not to argue.

"I get back to Missouri about once or twice a year. The folks still live on the farm I grew up on and my three brothers live nearby in town. My parents probably wouldn't be able to handle me visiting more often. It gets pretty raucous with all of us under one roof."

"Are any of your brothers married?"

"Only the oldest one, but my folks are still holding out hope for me and the twins." He grinned.

"Sounds like you all are close."

Jack nodded. "We are and I wouldn't have it any other way."

Delaney wasn't sure why she was surprised. Maybe part of her expected Jack to be estranged from his family due to his job...like she was. *Whose fault is that?* The same voice taunted. Delaney had felt so helpless after her sister was injured that she hadn't known what to do. That changed one career day on campus. It also changed her relationship with her parents—she hadn't had a real conversation with them since she'd walked into the house and told that that she was going into federal law enforcement.

"What about you?" he asked.

Silence stretched between them. Delaney didn't want to discuss her family, but she couldn't exactly ignore his question or he was bound to start getting suspicious. "My parents still live in Boston, along with my sister."

"Only one sibling?"

"Yes."

He stirred the vegetables. "Are you close?"

Delaney's throat tightened. "We used to be, but not so much anymore." She missed visiting with Elaine. They used to confide in each other, sharing secrets and laughter, along with their hopes and dreams. That ended with the gunshot. Her parents had become so over-protective that they pushed everyone away, including Delaney.

"It must be nice to be able to fly for free. You can get back to Boston for a visit anytime you like."

"Yeah, nice," she said absently.

"Your parents must be proud that you earned your wings."

Delaney tilted her head to look at him. "I wouldn't exactly say *proud* is the right word. They don't approve of my job." That wasn't exactly true. Her parents were proud of her, but they worried. Deep down Delaney knew they'd wanted her to pick something safer, something like Elaine would've picked before the accident.

They didn't understand that working in an office for a charitable organization would've driven her mad. She needed a job that melded with all the restless energy pulsing through her. The ATF had been a good fit physically. Too bad it wreaked havoc on her social life. Not many men outside of law enforcement wanted a girlfriend or a wife who carried a badge and a gun.

Jack frowned. "That's a shame. Maybe they'll change their minds after you've been flying for a while longer."

Delaney snorted. "I'm not holding my breath. What's with all the questions about flying, anyway?"

He didn't answer. Instead, Jack changed the subject. "If you hadn't mentioned it, I would've never guessed that you were an east coast girl. You have no accent."

She'd taken diction classes before joining the ATF to get rid of it, but Delaney couldn't say that. "I wanted to be an actress for a while. It's tough for people with thick accents not to be typecast." She mentally kicked herself for revealing one of her long-held dreams.

Why don't you tell him that you hate the color yellow, your birth sign is Gemini, you're an undercover agent with the ATF and that you want to jump his bones while you're at it?

She had wanted to be an actress while she was in high school. Her father had nixed that idea, dismissing it as frivolous, along with dancing, singing and painting. That was probably one of the reasons she enjoyed undercover work so much. It gave her a chance to allow the frustrated actress inside her the opportunity to play.

Her old man was from a different era. One where the roles of men and women were clearly defined. He thought he knew what was best for everyone, so he didn't bother with asking for an outside opinion. Delaney respected his feelings and tried to act like a proper young lady whenever she went home for a visit. She just wished that he appreciated her effort, instead of constantly finding fault with her and the choices that she'd made with her life.

So why didn't she feel like acting around Jack? Delaney didn't like the answer she received. She genuinely enjoyed his company. The man was utterly adorable in a 'can't have just one potato chip' kind of way. How many women had caved after gazing upon that smile? *Too many* was her guess. She wouldn't be joining their ranks.

They ate dinner and the conversation flowed naturally between them. Despite her reluctance, Delaney was drawn to his warmth and abundant charm. He laughed infectiously and was quick to smile. It was difficult to focus on the job with Jack regaling her with stories from his childhood. She found herself joining in, adding an anecdote here and there from her early years.

Finishing the meal, she pushed her plate aside. "That was delicious."

"Would you like some dessert or to take a tour of the house?" he asked, pushing his plate back. He didn't bother to hide the heat behind his gaze.

This was it. The chance to locate Jack's office. But from the look in his eyes, he had a lot more than a house tour in mind. How committed was she to breaking this case? Committed enough to go all the way? A physical relationship wasn't what her boss had in mind when he told her to get close to Jack. Delaney knew it and didn't bother to try to convince herself otherwise.

When she didn't answer, Jack added, "I could show you the house some other time."

Delaney took a big gulp of wine. Despite mixed feelings, she didn't want to leave. She wanted to break this case, but Delaney knew that wasn't the only reason she planned to take Jack up on his offer. Her growing attraction to him didn't have anything whatsoever to do with weapons, undercover work or promotions, and she was woman enough to admit it.

She wanted Jack, even if it were only for tonight. She wanted to know what it felt like to have him hold her in his arms, wrap his body around her, ride her gently into oblivion. Delaney nearly groaned at the thought.

She could chalk the whole thing up to the element of danger, but Delaney didn't make a habit of lying to herself. She may fib to the targets, but never to herself. She looked into Jack's eyes and felt a familiar spark. Whatever was happening between them on a biological level wasn't a lie and that would have to be enough for tonight. Tomorrow she could feel like a traitor to the cause.

"Let's go. We can have dessert later." Delaney set the wineglass down and signaled for him to lead the way.

THE BEAT OF Jack's heart pounded in his ears. Delaney looked as if she'd bolt at any second. He didn't want that to happen. Not when he was so close to taking her in his arms and lavishing her body with the loving attention it deserved. He longed to bury himself inside of her heat, until they were both too sated to move.

It was quite possible that she was the one woman he could confide in. The thought of having an honest relationship sent a thrill through Jack. He'd spent too many years pretending to be someone he wasn't, all so he could aid his country's allies and prevent enemies from becoming a global threat. Who'd have thought a fascination with weapons and a gift for selling could lead him down such a tangled road?

Dealing arms had started out innocently enough. He'd attended gun shows throughout college. On one such occasion, Jack had been speaking to a dealer who specialized in assault rifles. A customer had come up to peruse the merchandise. Jack found himself highlighting the weapon's features. The customer bought the rifle and Jack landed his first job in the business.

He'd worked his way up from there, moving to bigger and bigger dealers before eventually striking out on his own. There was a fine line between good and bad out in the field. He'd found that out the hard way. Jack had walked a very gray line and escaped the business while he was still able—unlike many of his colleagues. He'd managed to amass a small fortune in the process, which had allowed him to help out his parents with the farm and enter the art world.

He took a ragged breath, then sat his wineglass onto the counter, hoping Delaney didn't notice the trembling in his hands. She kept him perpetually off balance—a sensation he'd never experienced before.

One minute she smoldered, while the next, she could freeze water with a look. He'd received both, but the latter didn't deter him. If anything, it made Jack want to delve deeper. He sensed a passionate woman lurking beneath Delaney's calm exterior and he planned to coax her out, using everything in his sensual arsenal.

Something told him Delaney didn't normally sleep with a man on the first date, which made Jack beyond grateful that technically this could be considered their second. That didn't mean he could rush things, no matter how badly he wanted to strip the clothes away from her body.

Jack led Delaney down the hall, going room to room, but he chose to skip his office, a place he considered his personal domain. It held mementos he'd acquired over the years, including spent mortar casings. Not an easy thing to explain on a second date.

Her eyes strayed to the closed door, but he was determined to keep Delaney's attention focused on the artwork. He'd grown so used to the art being around that somewhere along the line he'd stopped looking at it. Showing the pieces to Delaney renewed his appreciation for the work and the woman.

He saved the master suite for last, throwing the thick double doors wide before stepping out of the way for Delaney to enter. Jack glanced around the room, following her gaze as she drank in the four-poster cherrywood bed in the center of the room, the custom fireplace in the corner, the city views out the wall of windows and the huge arch that led to the Italian marble master bath.

"What do you think?" For some reason her answer was important to him. He wanted her to like his home, feel comfortable here...*want to stay.*

"You like luxury." She scanned the room again.

"Yes, I do. I've come to appreciate a certain level of comfort."

"It's beautiful, like the rest of your home."

"Come. Sit." He led her across the room to the two chairs that flanked the fireplace. A rich Persian rug lay beneath their feet. Jack hit a button on the wall and flames burst from the hearth. "I love modern gadgets."

"I'm not very technically adept."

"No expertise needed with a switch and you don't have to get your hands dirty chopping wood."

She laughed. "I suppose that is a plus."

"Can I get you anything?" he asked, pointing to a discreet minifridge built into the wall.

"No, I'm fine. Thanks."

He pivoted to face her. "Delaney?"

"Yes." She tilted her head to look at him, her lashes concealing her emotions.

Jack couldn't seem to think straight. He stared at her for a moment, taking in her lush mouth and the angle of her stubborn chin, debating whether to reveal his past now instead of waiting. She didn't say anything, only continued to stare.

Delaney swallowed hard and moistened her bottom lip, sending his senses into high alert. Her brown gaze assessed him. Jack felt like something monumental hung in the balance. He'd give a Renoir to know what she was thinking.

Despite her natural openness, there was something about

Delaney Carson that seemed untouchable. Jack longed to know her secrets, explore her hidden alcoves. Perhaps they could both unburden their souls and share their secrets.

Her teeth clamped down on her lower lip and Jack nearly growled. He'd worry about exposing his past later. Right now, he had better things to do. He focused on her mouth and suddenly had to clear his dry throat.

"I would really like to kiss you," he said, his voice harsh. Jack curled his fingers into fists as he fought to keep from reaching for her. He needed her to come to him.

Delaney's luscious mouth opened forming a small *O*. Jack followed every nuance of her expression from her initial hesitation to her eventual capitulation. He didn't realize he'd been holding his breath until his lungs started to burn. He wanted this moment to be special for them both. Wanted her to want him as much as he desired her.

"What's stopping you?" she asked, challenge glinting in her mocha-colored eyes.

Relief washed the tension from his body. Her mouth widened into a smile that dared Jack to act.

Never one to back away from a challenge, he did.

7

ONCE JACK STARTED kissing Delaney he knew it would be a long time, if ever, before he'd want to stop. His mouth melded to hers, and he separated her lips with his tongue, before plunging inside to taste her sweetness. A hint of red wine lingered in her depths, adding tang to her evocative flavor. He chased the elusive essence, exploring her thoroughly. It was even better than the night before, richer, more invested. Or maybe he was. Jack wasn't sure.

He cupped the back of Delaney's neck with one hand, bringing her closer to him. He caressed the column of her throat, feeling her pulse jump under his fingertips as he devoured her. Something about this woman brought out the caveman in Jack. He wanted to drag her off by her hair until she agreed to stay with him. The thought should scare him, but it didn't. For some reason, it felt right. She felt right.

His heart pounded in his chest as his hands slid over her shoulders and onto her breasts. Small, tight and compact, Delaney's nipples hardened, stabbing his palms as he flicked the crests with his thumbs. He couldn't wait to see her, taste her, drive her completely out of her mind with pleasure. Then when Jack finished, he'd start all over again. Delaney whimpered and tried to pull away.

He stopped, even though it pained him to do so. Jack rested his forehead on hers. "We don't have to do anything tonight, if you aren't ready," he said, staring at her kiss swollen lips.

"No, I want to." She met his gaze. "I want this." Her fingers trembled as she moved to the buttons on the front of her shirt.

"Allow me." Jack brushed Delaney's hand aside and began to unbutton her blouse slowly. Inch by excruciating inch revealed more pale flesh to his overheated senses. A demure lace bra supported her modest portions. With a flick of his wrist, Jack bared her. She was beautiful, just like he knew she'd be. Peach-colored crescents over creamy mounds. The urge to taste nearly brought him to his knees.

Delaney's questing fingers reached under his shirt, then pulled it over his head, before dropping it onto the chair beside them. Jack growled and lowered his mouth, moving first to one peaked nipple, and then the other. So sweet. Succulent. And unlike anything he'd ever encountered. One taste wasn't nearly enough.

He kneaded her breasts, while sucking her deep within the warmth of his mouth. Jack flicked his tongue and her breath staggered. The utterly feminine sound spurred him on. He needed to fill her, lose himself inside her. The thought of Delaney's moist channel cradling him as he thrust in and out of her sent Jack's hunger into overdrive. He knew without question that one night with Delaney Carson would never be enough.

She was exactly what he'd been searching for since he'd left the farm in Missouri. Never one to second guess his instincts, Jack knew beyond a doubt that Delaney would fit right in with his family. He also knew that if he admitted as much to her that it would scare her away. So he vowed to take it slow.

THE TREMBLING STARTED at the base of Delaney's spine and spread upward, before plummeting. She'd planned to keep her distance, but her mind wasn't cooperating. Her knees wobbled, threatening to buckle, but Jack held her steady, while he lowered his head and feasted upon her breasts. Delaney had heard of women who could orgasm this way, but she wasn't one of them.

Or at least she hadn't thought she was until Jack touched her. The fact that she was so close to orgasm reminded her it had been way too long since she'd last had sex. Delaney told herself it had nothing to do with Jack. She'd be like this with any man. The lie slid easily into her thoughts. Too bad she didn't buy it.

Her body thrummed in anticipation. They both still wore their pants, though somehow they'd managed to toe off their shoes. The silk of his hair brushed across her collarbone as he paid homage to her breasts.

Her head dropped back as she brought her hands up to cradle his face. Without thought, Delaney drew him closer, holding him against her flesh in encouragement. The heat of his mouth coupled with the scrape of his teeth left her gasping for air. Gone was the gentleman who'd graciously given her a tour of his home. He'd been replaced by a primal being who was currently devouring her alive.

And she was a willing sacrifice.

Delaney sunk her fingers into his hair, raking his scalp as she tried to pull him up. She needed to taste his lips again, feel the slide of his tongue as he breached her mouth repeatedly.

Jack had the most amazing lips that delivered toe-curling kisses.

He released her nipple, then began blazing a trail down her abdomen. Jack dropped to one knee, his tongue circling her navel before dipping inside. She flinched in surprise.

"That tickles," Delaney said, playfully slapping him on the shoulder.

"I'll file that away for later." Jack chuckled, then did it again.

"Hey," she said.

"Okay, I'll stop…for now." Jack held Delaney's hips to control her movements. He took her zipper between his teeth and slowly worked it down. His blue eyes remained locked on her face all the while. Delaney groaned at the sight of him, kneeling before her with passion smoldering in his expression.

Warmth flooded her face, joining the moisture that trickled between her thighs. Jack reached for the button holding her pants together. He slipped it out of its hole. Her slacks gaped in a wide V, exposing the lace of her underwear. Before she could move or even think, Jack buried his nose in the lacey front and inhaled, sliding her trousers down her legs at the same time.

His tongue flicked out, wetting the front of her sex as her pants hit the floor. "Do you have any idea how wonderful you smell to me? Hot, spicy and wholly feminine. You make my head spin."

Delaney couldn't get her vocal cords to work, so she shook her head. He murmured something unintelligible and reached for the lace, hooking it at the sides with two fingers. She stilled his hands before he could remove the tiny scrap of material.

"I think it's your turn," she said, tugging his arms until he stood before her.

"And here I thought I was about to uncover a buried treasure." The blue of his eyes had nearly disappeared as hunger etched his masculine face.

Delaney unbuckled his belt. She slid the leather from the loops with a small hiss, dropping the belt onto his shirt in the chair. Her gaze flicked to the bulge behind his zipper a second before she boldly stroked the hard ridge of his erection.

The breath rushed from Jack's lungs as enough she wrapped her hands around his length and began to pump his flesh. The velvet softness of him pulsed and grew beneath her fingertips.

"If you keep that up this is going to be a real short night." He gasped.

Delaney grinned and kept caressing him. Jack's hips bucked and he let out a strangled moan. "I'll take my chances," she said undoing the clasp of his pants. She took her hand away long enough to lower his zipper. He wasn't wearing any underwear. "Come prepared, do we?"

"Darlin', I'm a regular Boy Scout."

She stroked him again, feeling the velvet softness of his engorged flesh.

"Don't say I didn't warn you," Jack uttered between clenched teeth. He kicked his pants away, then lifted Delaney off the floor, carrying her to the massive bed with ease.

Delaney squealed in surprise, but hung on, grasping Jack's broad shoulders, while glorying in the feel of his naked body caressing hers. He laid her down carefully, despite the urgency she could feel coursing beneath his fingers. Gently still, he removed her underwear. Once he finished, Jack stepped back and stared, drinking in her nakedness.

Normally shy, for some reason Delaney relished his attention. It was like truly seeing herself for the first time.

"You are beautiful." His eyes smoldered and for a second she thought he was about to say more. But Delaney would barely concentrate on his words. He was lying beside her now, and starting at her neck, Jack stroked the length of her torso, his hand barely touching her skin.

Goose bumps rose over her flesh. He paused at the nest of curls between her thighs, then lightly threaded his fingers through the mass until he reached her clit. Delaney nearly came off the bed when he flicked the erect bundle of nerves with his thumbnail.

She grasped the comforter beneath her, fisting the material to anchor her body. Her breath came out in pants as Jack continued to pleasure her. He slowly lowered his mouth to one breast and began to suck in time with each caress. Delaney let out a keening cry and her body bowed as an orgasm ripped through her.

Before the ripples could fade, Jack plunged one finger inside of her, curling it until his knuckle brushed the hidden nerves inside. Delaney's hips thrust against the invasion. She closed her eyes as a second wave of sensation rolled her in bliss.

"Oh, Jack," she murmured as the current pulled her under.

Had she ever responded to a man like this? Delaney knew the answer before the question finished forming. There was something about Jack that was different. She hated to admit it, but he was unique. Damn him.

"You are so tight and wet," he murmured against her skin. "It's been a while for you, hasn't it?"

"One year, six days—" she lifted her head to look at the clock next to his bed "—eight hours and ten minutes, but who's counting?"

Jack laughed around her nipple, but refused to release her aching flesh. "I guess—" *lick* "—we'll have to—" *flick* "—do something—" *suck* "—about that tonight." *Nuzzle*.

"You're driving me crazy. You know that, right?"

He grinned, then nipped her. "I'm not done yet." To emphasize his words, Jack slipped a second finger inside of her and twisted his wrist until he could stroke in and out.

"I shouldn't feel this much so soon," she gasped. "I think I'm going to—"

"That's it," he coaxed, pressing down on her clit.

"Jack." His name was a plea and invocation all in one. She threw her head back and shuddered hard. Delaney saw stars behind her eyelids as her body convulsed in the best orgasm she'd ever experienced.

Never in all her years of dating had she reached release this often or quickly and they hadn't even had intercourse yet. The thought caused her body to tighten in anticipation.

"Lovely." Jack's voice cracked as he pressed butterfly kisses on her glistening skin.

He stroked her curls soothingly as she rode out the last waves of her release. Delaney heard a drawer open and close, then the sound of foil ripping. Warm, male musk surrounded her. Jack sheathed himself, then kissed her eyelids, nose and cheeks, before seeking her mouth. His body slid over hers, his welcoming weight pressing her down into the soft comforter. He parted her thighs with the brush of his knee.

Moisture wept from her center as the tip of his shaft kissed her opening, then slipped inside. Hard, heavy and thick, he rocked his hips, driving his cock deeper. Delaney whimpered as her body adjusted to his impressive size.

She opened her eyes and their gazes collided and locked. In that moment, there were no lies, no case, no Jack and Delaney…only a man and his woman doing what they were put on this planet to do. Delaney fought the feeling, but it was too strong. Something rose within her, then melted, fusing them together.

Sweat beaded Jack's brow and tension lined his jaw. Muscles in his arms quivered as he kept the bulk of his weight off her, while he thrust forward, burying himself to the hilt. He groaned as he increased the tempo.

Bodies joined in motion, Delaney met him stroke for stroke. Her fingers dug into the flesh of his shoulder, before sliding down his back to grip his tight ass. Jack flexed beneath her fingertips, then he pulled her legs over his hips.

"Keep them there," he panted, his breath coming in quick gasps. "Delaney, you feel so good. I wish we could stay like this forever, but I don't think I'm going to last much longer."

He rocked her, drawing out a moan from between her

parted lips. The sensations were too much. She clung to Jack as he rolled his hips, fanning her need to match his own. Somewhere between the fireplace and the bed, Delaney had stopped acting.

She wasn't doing this for the job. She was doing this because she wanted to know what it felt like to lie beneath Jack Gordon, feel his scorching kisses and taste the salt of his sweat as she raked her teeth across his steely body.

Jack's groans turned to primal grunts.

"Now, Jack, now," Delaney cried out.

His hand slipped between their bodies and stroked her clit. Blood roared in Delaney's ears as she flew apart. Jack thrust once, twice, and then bellowed as he reached for and found his release.

They lay wrapped in each others' arms, their breathing labored, as they slowly floated back to reality. The awkwardness that had existed between them now slept peacefully.

"Thank you," he said, kissing her eyelids.

"For what?"

"For giving me the gift of your body tonight."

"Jack…"

He kissed her into silence.

The heat of their sweat-soaked skin radiated between them like a living, breathing entity.

"I have a confession to make," he said.

Delaney tensed. She didn't want to hear anything that might take away from this moment, but had little choice in the matter. "Go ahead," she said.

"I've wanted to do this since I first laid eyes on you," he murmured. Jack kissed a trail over her cheek and onto her neck, where he proceeded to nuzzle her ear.

She shuddered as a sensual aftershock rumbled though her. "You keep doing that and I'll want a repeat performance."

Jack nipped her lobe before soothing it with his tongue. "That can be arranged, but I'd better get cleaned up first." He pulled out of her body, leaving an acute loss of warmth behind.

Delaney watched him cross the room, mesmerized by his naked backside. Jack glanced over his shoulder and winked at her before slipping into the bathroom. She heard a faucet turn on, the water splashing. He returned a few minutes later sans the condom.

"Are you okay?" he asked, slipping into bed beside her. He tenderly brushed the side of her head with his fingertips. Delaney didn't miss the slight tremble in his hands or the caring cast to his eyes. She wanted so much for all this to be real.

"I'm good. You?"

Jack kissed Delaney's forehead. "Couldn't be better. Just waiting for my body to give me the go-ahead for round two."

Delaney elbowed him playfully in his side. Jack made an *oomph* sound, catching her arm at the same time.

"What was that for?"

"You were supposed to say something flattering or tender."

"I thought I had." He chuckled.

"Don't you know the rules?" She cocked her head to look at him, unable to keep the smile from her face.

"Apparently not. Why don't you fill me in…or better yet, why don't I fill you in," he said, rolling her beneath him.

THEY MADE LOVE throughout the night, sometimes tenderly and sometimes with such a fierce need that it actually frightened Delaney. Neither noticed the van parked down the hill or heard the buzz of the tiny camera at the window as it recorded their every move.

JACK FELL ASLEEP shortly before dawn. He lay under the covers, his chest bare and an arm thrown across his face.

Earlier, he'd given her one of his shirts to wear, the material soft and warm against her skin.

Delaney pressed a sleeve into her nose and inhaled. She could smell Jack in the fabric. For a second, she considered taking the shirt for a keepsake, but then decided against it. How immature would that be?

She watched the steady rise and fall of Jack's gorgeous abdomen. The muscles rippled beneath his taut skin. Delaney had the overwhelming urge to reach out and stroke his tousled hair. It had felt like silk last night against her fingertips and she longed to feel it again.

She glanced around the huge master suite, recalling their evening together. Jack Gordon was without a doubt the most considerate lover she'd ever had. He was also intelligent, witty and wickedly delightful to be around. Guilt sank its talons in and ripped at Delaney's gut. Did she care nothing for her duty, her family? What had she been thinking?

Even as she asked herself the last question, Delaney already knew the answer. She hadn't been thinking at all. Instead she'd turned into an insatiable tactile creature, who couldn't get enough of this man.

There had been times during the night when her heart had rejoiced at finding Jack, only to weep under the circumstances. It would be so easy to fall for him. A tiny part of her already had. Yet there was no way this could end happily.

Delaney swallowed the resentment rising in her throat. "Why did you have to be an arms dealer, Jack? Of all things," she murmured under her breath. And just like that, something that felt suspiciously like hope crumbled inside Delaney.

She slipped from the bed silently, keeping one eye on Jack as she inched toward her purse. It had ended up on the floor next to her clothes. Jack snuffled and she froze. What felt like an eternity later, he seemed to settle into a deeper sleep.

Delaney released the breath she'd been holding and grabbed her purse. She rummaged through the bottom until she found the USB drive she'd brought with her. She grabbed the tiny key drive, then put her purse back on the rug. Delaney crept across the floor to the bedroom door and turned the handle, thanking the heavens that it opened on a whisper.

She took a deep breath and gave one last look at Jack. Even with bed-ruffled hair and sheet marks imprinted in his cheek, he was still the most gorgeous guy she'd ever laid eyes on. The chances of her meeting someone like him in the future were slim to never going to happen. What a pity.

Delaney shut the door behind her, ignoring the sadness welling inside of her. She made her way to the one room Jack hadn't shown her on his tour last night. Delaney turned the knob and the door creaked.

She cursed under her breath, glancing at the double doors at the end of the hall that led to the master bedroom. Thank goodness they remained closed. She pushed aside a sudden bout of guilt, then stepped into the room, shutting the door behind her.

A mahogany desk stood in the center of the room with paper strewn atop it. Dim light filtered through the closed plantation shutters on the window. Overflowing bookcases lined the walls. On top of them, she noted a couple of spent mortar casings. A silent reminder of why she was here.

A laptop sat in the middle of the desk, the screen saver morphing clouds into various shapes. A filing cabinet flanked the desk. Delaney walked across the lush carpet to the window. She tilted the shutters to allow more light to spill into the room, then moved to the desk.

The antique desk only had two drawers, which contained basic office supplies and nothing more. Delaney frowned. She woke his computer. It didn't appear to have password-protected files. If Jack had information about the sale or movement of arms, this would be where he'd keep it.

So why wasn't she finding anything?

She scanned his files, then slipped the USB drive into the unit and downloaded as many files as she could from his hard drive. It took a couple of minutes.

Delaney placed the USB drive into her shirt pocket, then moved to a filing cabinet. There were no locks. She opened the top drawer. It held typical office paperwork such as taxes, insurance information and deeds. The second cabinet drawer seemed to be dedicated to his art purchases.

Had he really retired? If so, what was he transporting on the plane in the briefcase that he didn't want anyone else to touch?

Delaney shut the filing cabinet drawer and flipped the shades down, plunging the room back into shadows. Myriad emotions filled her as she walked the short distance to the door. She should be relieved that she hadn't been able to find proof of his criminal activity related to the case at hand, but Delaney wasn't. It still didn't change what she had to do. Somehow, she had to get Jack's cooperation or there was a good possibility innocent people would die.

She opened the door and stepped out into the hall. Jack stood against the opposite wall with his arms crossed over his bare chest and one leg propped behind him. He'd slipped on a pair of dove-gray sweatpants, but hadn't bothered to tie them. Worry weathered his features, pulling his lips into a thin line.

"What were you doing?"

"I—I was looking for the bathroom," she sputtered, knowing he'd never believe the lie. Hell, she wouldn't in his place.

His expression remained cold, but something flared behind his eyes. *Was that hurt?*

"There's one attached to the bedroom, if you hadn't

noticed." He stalked down the hall toward the kitchen without another word, his back ramrod-straight.

Delaney's heart trampled her ribs. She closed her eyes a second, berating herself for being talked in to taking this assignment. Her nose caught the aroma of brewing coffee, and she opened her eyes. Moments later, she'd calmed down enough to enter the kitchen. Jack held a mug in his hands, while staring out the window at the valley below.

Another mug waited for her on the counter, steam rising from the contents. Cream and sugar sat nearby. Delaney cringed inwardly as she padded forward over the cool tiles. This situation would be so much easier if he just screamed at her. Instead, he was back to acting like the perfect gentleman, which made her feel even worse.

This was the first time Delaney had really hated her job.

"You know, for some reason," he said, turning toward her, "I thought it was the male attendant who'd planted this on me." He pushed the GPS chip across the counter with one finger, stopping when it was right in front of her.

Delaney glanced down at the device and winced. She picked up her coffee and took a sip, trying hard to swallow the acrid substance around the lump in her throat. She was only doing her job.

He continued. "I thought there was no way the government would assign someone so obviously out of their depth as you are on a plane, to follow me." He paused, his hurt gaze jumping to her face. "Unless that was an act, too...like last night. Is Delaney Carson even your real name?"

"Delaney is real."

"But not Carson."

"No." She shook her head.

His jaw clenched. "I really have to hand it to you, Delaney, you had me fooled. I never met anyone who could orgasm on cue, or were you faking it? Either way, you deserve an award for that performance."

She flinched. "Jack."

"Don't," he growled under his breath, before running a hand through his hair, sending dark strands in all directions. "This is low, even for the feds."

"Let me explain."

He laughed, but the noise sounded pained. "How can you possibly explain all this?" He waved his hand in the air to encompass the room.

"We need your help."

He snorted. "*We?* Which branch of the government do you work for anyway?"

Delaney's hands shook so bad that she needed to put her cup down. "I work for the Department of Alcohol, Tobacco, Firearms and Explosives."

"Of course you do," Jack said, sarcasm lacing his voice as he refilled his cup. He held the pot in the air and shook it, nodding to her.

"No, thank you."

He sat the pot down and moved back to the window. "I hope you got a good laugh. I can't believe I was stupid enough to think you might be special."

Delaney paused, the emotional blow more painful than she'd anticipated. "Jack, please, hear me out."

"Why should I? You've been playing me this whole time."

She moved toward him. "Because if you don't, a lot of innocent people are going to die."

He glanced at her. "That's not my problem."

"You know, if you'd have said that yesterday, I might have believed you actually meant it. But not now. I know you…at least a little."

Jack glared at her. "You don't know anything about me."

"Yes, I do," Delaney whispered.

"No, you don't...." His voice trailed off.

She blanched, his words scoring her conscience. "I'm sorry."

"Yeah, me, too," he murmured as he stared down into his coffee.

"We still need your help."

Jack spun to face her. "I'm retired, out of the business. Don't you people get that?"

She knew he had every right to be angry. If their roles were reversed, Delaney would be livid. "According to our sources, someone is bringing in a large shipment of weapons this week into Los Angeles. Our intelligence tells us there's enough firepower to take out a small U.S. city or start a private war. We have to stop them," she said.

He curled his hands into fists, then straightened his fingers, before running his palms over his stubbled face. "I was never involved with that side. Everything I sold was legal."

Delaney wanted to believe him, but it didn't change the fact that the guns he sold ended lives. "You sold to enemies of the United States." The words pained her to say, even if it was the truth.

He shook his head. "You don't understand. They weren't always our enemies. Check your dates and facts. I think you'll find that to be the case."

In her mind, there had never been a difference, since all she saw on the job was the destruction these weapons wreaked. She realized that to Jack there was a difference, a big difference. "We've checked you out thoroughly. Apparently, you are incredibly gifted at covering your tracks and hiding your assets. So much so, that we can't tell if you've been doing anything illegal. That was one of the things I was sent in to find out."

"You really don't know anything about the sale of weapons, do you?"

Slightly embarrassed from her lack of knowledge, Delaney shook her head.

"It's a lucrative business when you're legal, even more so if you deal illegally. The business is dangerous either route you take, but I was damn good at it. I took the money I earned and invested it in art, property and technology. Not that it's any of your business."

"Okay." Delaney leaned against the kitchen sink. "Say I believe you. That doesn't mean that you don't know who would bring in a shipment."

"I might, but I'm not about to get involved in this again. I got out and I'm staying out. The business is tricky. After the Berlin Wall came down it got even trickier. I was lucky to walk away with my fortune and health intact. I go back and there's a good possibility I'll end up dead. The men and women who work in the business aren't exactly the most stable individuals."

Delaney's stomach dropped. The thought of Jack coming to harm made her ill. How could she have thought he was expendable?

She knew that McMillan specifically stated that Jack was their best hope in helping them and that the Bureau would provide protection if necessary. McMillan wouldn't send an agent in unless a threat to Jack's welfare had been verified. At the time, Delaney had agreed given his line of work, but now...

Without Jack's insight and given the circumstances, she'd have to find another way to stop this shipment.

"So everything you told me last night about being a flight attendant was a lie?" he asked, surprising her.

Delaney couldn't look at him. "Not exactly."

Jack stepped forward and lifted his hand as if to touch her, then seemed to think better of it. "You really don't like to fly, do you?"

"No." She shook her head.

"So you alluded to one truth. I wonder how many more you told during your fancy deception." Jack took a sip of coffee and stared at her, his expression unreadable. "What do you get out of this deal?"

Delaney shrugged. "The satisfaction of knowing that I've saved lives."

"That's very noble, but what do you personally get out of this deal?"

"A promotion."

He cocked his head. "Seems to me that if you've gone to all this trouble it's for more than an elevation of status or a sense of duty. I'd say you have something to prove. The question is to who?"

"Are you going to help us or not?" she asked, trying to divert Jack's questions, which were getting far too close to home.

"I can't," he said, pouring more coffee. "I'm sorry."

"I understand. I'll get my things and leave." She paused, admitting she really didn't want to go.

Jack turned his back to her. "You know, Delaney, you didn't have to fuck me to find out what I was up to. All you had to do was ask."

8

THE COVERS ON THE BED were in disarray and the room still held the odor of delicious sex. Delaney stared at the twisted sheets for a moment, reliving the rush of last night's encounter. Despite the fact that Jack Gordon was her assignment, she'd never jumped into bed with a man this fast. And she'd never, ever slept with a target in order to garner their cooperation. Actually, she hadn't slept with a target, period... other than Jack.

She shook her head and then went to gather her clothes. Delaney dropped the USB drive into her purse, then reached for the end of Jack's shirt and pulled it over her head. She heard a sharp intake of breath behind her and spun.

Jack stood in the doorway, his hand gripping the knob as he stared, transfixed at her naked body. He didn't bother to hide the desire that flared to life in his eyes or the anger. Warmth spread into her abdomen. She folded her arms across her chest, feeling suddenly vulnerable. Jack stepped into the room and shut the door.

"What are you going to do now?" he asked nonchalantly as he made the bed.

Delaney dressed quickly, unable to meet his gaze. She thought about his question for a few moments, and then finally answered. "Since you turned me down, I have no choice but to move to the second man on the list."

Jack stiffened. "Are you going to sleep with him, too?"

"Of course not." Her head jerked and their eyes clashed. "Contrary to what you believe, I do not make a habit of sleeping with my *assignments*. I wasn't lying when I said it's been over a year for me."

Delaney wasn't sure what Jack saw in her expression, but he seemed to relax a fraction.

"So who's second on the list?" He tucked the sheet under the mattress.

"It's not important."

He grasped a pillow and punched it before tossing it back onto the bed. "Suit yourself. I thought I could see if I recognized the name. The players change frequently."

Delaney considered his words. She doubted that Jack would warn the man and she couldn't see any obvious complications from giving him the knowledge. "David Rico," she said finally, pulling her shoes on.

ALREADY REELING from the news that he'd been deceived, Jack froze midmotion the second Delaney said the man's name. He'd never personally worked with Rico, but he *had* heard of him. Or more to the point, heard about his reputation for sudden bouts of violence.

"I think you should reconsider. Rico takes no prisoners and plays rough. He has one of the worst reputations for brutality in the business. Are you sure you can handle him?"

Delaney glanced at Jack. "Yes."

"Like you did me?" He hated to ask, hated the jealousy he heard in his voice. She'd already claimed otherwise, but he needed to hear it again to soothe the anger and hurt scalding his insides. If she'd sleep with anyone to get ahead, then he'd gladly walk away, but he didn't think that was the case. At least he hoped not.

He refused to believe that he was that wrong about her. Despite her deception, Jack felt as if he'd gotten a glimpse of the true Delaney last night. The one who enjoyed giving and receiving pleasure. The one who laughed at his stupid jokes and who couldn't catch a pepper with her mouth.

She shook her head. "Things got out of hand. I should've stopped before we..."

Jack's face flushed. There was no way in hell he was going to let her dismiss what they'd shared last night. Despite the lies and deceptions, he knew in his gut that they'd connected. His gut never lied. All he had to do now was convince Delaney, but that would have to wait until they'd cleared the air.

"Rico will smell you coming a mile away, and when he does, there won't be enough of you left to identify the body," he said tersely, wanting her to understand what she was dealing with.

Delaney folded his shirt and stepped close enough to lay it on the bed, but still far enough to remain out of his reach. What did she think he was going to do? Did she truly think he was some kind of monster after everything they'd experienced?

"Are you trying to scare me?" she asked, her expression growing wary.

"No, I'm trying to keep you from doing something incredibly stupid."

"Don't worry about me, Jack. I'm a big girl and a trained professional agent. I can take care of myself."

Jack stepped forward and grabbed Delaney's chin, tilting it until their eyes met. Desire flared. Her skin burned his fingertips, but he refused to release her.

"This isn't a game, Delaney. David Rico is a killer and smart enough to not get caught. If he's involved in the shipment you're talking about, the ATF will need more than you to stop him. From what I've heard, the man has enough ammo to hold off an army and has a paramilitary group at his disposal."

She twisted until she slipped out of his grasp. "We're not sure Rico's involved, he's still a question mark. Right now, we need all the information we can get. We thought you could supply the names of the most likely individuals behind the deal. If we knew who was running this shipment, we might be able to infiltrate their operation and stop them before the sale goes through. At least that was the plan, but obviously we were wrong."

Guilt clutched him. Though damned if Jack knew why. "I'm not the one who deceived you, remember? It was the other way around." Jack realized the irony of the situation as he spoke.

"I have to do what I can. The stakes are too high to walk away."

"Listen, it could be David Rico, and you can't just waltz into this life and expect to remain unscathed. If his suspicions are raised, the man will strike when you least expect it."

Delaney stared right at him. Hard. "You've turned me down. What choice do I have?"

Jack knew what he was about to do was utter insanity, but for some reason couldn't bring himself to stop. There was no way he'd ever allow her to approach David Rico alone. It was suicide, even if she didn't believe him. His mind flashed to the bodies of the people he couldn't save, the deals that had gone bad for no apparent reason. He might not have been there for them, but he could be there for Delaney.

What was he thinking?

The woman used him, lied to him and betrayed him. Still, he couldn't bring himself to let her go. What was the matter with him? If he had any sense, he'd tell her goodbye and be done with it. The sex had been good, but it wasn't *that* good. Okay, maybe it was, but it wasn't worth dying over.

No, but she is.

Jack stilled at the revelation. How had Delaney gotten

under his skin so quickly? Their entire meeting was based on carefully orchestrated lies. Well, not all lies. Jack had managed to ascertain that much from their conversation in the kitchen. Whether she realized it or not, Delaney had confided in him. She'd shared a part of herself that he doubted few ever saw, if any.

For some reason, that small concession made all the difference in the world to Jack. It meant that maybe when this mess was all over they'd actually have a chance. Despite everything that had happened, he wanted that chance. He'd been around long enough to recognize something special when he saw it. And Delaney, with all her foibles, was special. They were special together. Jack hoped they lived long enough for him to convince her.

"I can help you get close to David Rico." He tensed as the words slipped from his taut lips.

She frowned. "But you said—"

"I know what I said and I've changed my mind."

Her brown eyes narrowed to slits. "Why?"

He wasn't prepared to explain what he didn't fully understand himself. "The reason isn't important."

She crossed her arms and struck an obstinate pose. "It is to me."

Jack shook his head, strolling over to his bedroom window. Paradise Valley, the Beverly Hills of Arizona, glittered in the sunlight like a fine jewel sitting in the sands. "Let's just say, I'd prefer that you not be turned into shark bait."

"Swimming with the fishes? Isn't that a bit clichéd?". Delaney's quip had Jack turning around.

"Perhaps, but in this instance, it's also an apt description." Despite her bravado, he could see the relief in her face.

She grinned at him in a wholly female "I got what I wanted" kind of way.

Jack cursed under his breath, then calmed as a plan formed in his mind. He needed a way of keeping Delaney close until he could convince her there was more between them than sex. "You may not be smiling after you hear my terms for this tentative agreement."

Her smile slowly faded. "I knew there had to be a catch."

It was Jack's turn to grin. "Isn't there always?" He watched her squirm as she waited for him to explain. She deserved to sweat after what she'd done.

Her face mottled as her impatience grew. He stifled a cough. "If we do this, you're no longer in charge of the operation. I am."

Something dangerous glittered in her brown eyes. Jack wasn't sure what response he hoped to see. If she knew what was good for her, Delaney would return to the ATF office and request to be replaced. What was she trying to prove?

Delaney's comments about her family filtered through his mind. He understood more than most the need to make your parents proud. His folks hadn't exactly cheered when he'd come home and told them that he was a legal arms dealer.

Like any parents, they worried about his safety. He'd told them what had happened at the gun show and said it was a chance to learn the business, while helping his country. The latter had eventually been what sold his parents on the idea. They were patriotic enough to agree that his job was needed.

Would the need for parental approval be enough to make Delaney risk her physical safety? He looked her way and had his answer.

Jack glanced at his reflection in the window and noted the tension in his face. A year away from the business and he'd somehow forgotten everything he'd learned about confronting adversaries. Jack forced himself to relax.

"I don't think I can allow you to run the operation," she said.

He shrugged. "Take it or leave it."

"Why do you have to be in charge?"

"Because you *used* me. More importantly, I know the business."

Delaney began to pace the width of the bed. She muttered under her breath, shaking her head and nodding in equal parts. Jack watched with amusement as an entire conversation took place without him. He would've laughed if he thought Delaney could hear him, but she was off in her own little world.

"Are you finished, because there is more?" he asked softly as a shiver snaked its way down her spine. "In order to get close to David Rico a couple of things have to occur. First, I have to convince the top people that I'm back in the game or, better yet, that I never left. Second, we have to befriend Rico."

"Exactly how are we supposed to do that?" She set her purse onto the bed.

"Your agency can handle the first part. I'll take care of the latter."

She stopped and frowned, looking around the room as if it were the first time she'd seen it. "I'll have to check with a few people. I'm not senior enough to make these kinds of decisions."

"Then I suggest you do that right away. This offer is non-negotiable and only available for a limited time." He took a step toward her.

She stiffened, but didn't move away.

"One more thing." Jack leaned his face close until the warmth of his breath caressed her cheek. The pulse beat wildly in Delaney's throat as her gaze locked onto his mouth. Jack wanted to taste her so bad it hurt, but he needed to get the last of his terms out beforehand. "I want the ATF's assurance that after I do this they will drop any and all investigations against me."

Delaney was silent, then her nostrils flared. "You're not asking for much," she said, sarcasm dripping from her words.

"And here I thought I was being very reasonable."

She snorted.

Jack stared at her upturned face and fought the urge to pull her into his embrace. Delaney had an innocence about her that called to him. It made Jack want to protect her, hold her, keep her. The last thought made him inwardly flinch, even as he accepted it as the truth. He doubted Delaney would appreciate the sentiment.

"Your people need to get word out on the street that I had a major deal go down."

He glanced at her again, falling into her eyes, drowning in the warm molasses depths. Jack had sated himself in her body several times throughout the night. How could he still be so hungry? He tamped down his desire and returned to the business at hand. "Rico has a fascination with fast cars and boats. The bigger the boat, the better. It might be a way to get to him."

She laughed. "Some people would call that overcompensating for something."

"I wouldn't know."

Delaney's gaze dropped to the front of his sweats and he felt himself respond instantly. "No, I don't suppose you would."

Jack turned to hide his smile. "My point is that I happen to own a *modest*-sized boat."

"How modest?"

"Forty-three feet."

Delaney choked. "Forty-three feet? That's a cruise ship, not a boat. I would hate to hear what you consider high-end." She stared for a moment, then seemed to snap out of her surprise.

"You think you can tempt David Rico with the opportunity to sail on it."

"You don't sail on a Wellcraft Forty-three Scarab AVS with custom finishing, darling. You fly."

"Whatever." She rolled her eyes and shook her head. "Just answer the question."

"Maybe." Jack shrugged. "You never know. Rico's always in the market for a new toy. He likes to have the latest technology, but the toy doesn't have to be a boat." He gave her a quick once-over.

"Great." She smirked. "I guess that takes care of your part. Now where do I come in to the picture? I do still get to be part of *my* case, right?"

"Certainly," Jack glanced at her, his gaze raking her body. "Like most men, David Rico has an appreciation for the feminine form."

"Okay, so you'll introduce me on the boat. I'll flirt and try to get close to him."

"No!" Jack's jaw clenched and he took a step back, reeling from the sudden possessive feelings that tightened his chest. When had he ever worried about a woman? *Never*.

He'd always kept his relationships open-ended so that either party could walk at anytime. Jack told himself it was just that he hadn't sated his lust for her yet. He took a calming breath. "We don't know if he's going to be interested yet. And we don't want to be too obvious or he'll get suspicious. It's not like I'm still in the game."

She scowled. "These sound like stall tactics, Jack. I told you that I'll try to get you everything you've asked for. There's no need to delay this meet. I would think you'd be happy that I've agreed to negotiate."

Happy? Was she insane? What was there to be happy about? In all likelihood David Rico would kill them both, then dump their bodies out at sea. Jack grit his teeth. "Rico doesn't do business with women. He believes they're only good for one thing."

"One thing?" Delaney's look of recognition stopped him cold. "Is that what you believe?"

Jack didn't answer. Not because he agreed with Rico—he didn't. But there was a primitive part of him that wanted, or worse yet, needed to protect a woman. He may not be exactly Stone Age in his thinking, but he hadn't quite moved into the twenty-first century, either.

He worshipped the feminine form with its soft curves and delicate valleys. He relished Delaney's quick mind and acerbic wit. He knew women were perfectly capable of doing any job there was. That said, he wasn't about to let Delaney get anywhere near Rico without him.

"Men," she muttered under her breath. "What do you expect me to do while you're playing with the big boys?"

Jack arched a brow and grinned. "You are going to play the part of my girlfriend. I hope you own a bikini."

"A bikini? Have you lost your mind?" She looked mutinous.

Jack straightened. "We may have to work on the girlfriend aspect." He stroked his chin and eyed her, imagining stilettos strapped to Delaney's feet, a short leather skirt hugging her hips and a corset cinching in her trim waist. Not exactly boat gear, but definitely one of his fantasies.

His gaze started at her feet, then slowly worked its way up, pausing at her nipples, which hardened beneath her shirt, before he continued to her rosey face.

Jack's heartbeat jackknifed and his breathing grew shallow as he imagined her in an extra tiny black bikini. All that pale bare skin exposed and waiting to be stroked. From what he'd seen last night, Delaney's legs weren't extraordinarily long, but they were toned like the rest of her body.

He'd loved every inch of her and wouldn't mind a repeat performance. His shaft rose to full mast. He turned away to adjust his sweats before facing her once more.

Jack cleared his throat and forced his mind to focus. "You have to understand something about David Rico. He doesn't play by your rules. Rumor has it the guy's a psycho. An extremely paranoid psycho. I heard that he shot one of his own people once because he was bored. Pretending to be an unassuming female is the only way Rico will allow you to hang around him."

She glanced down and shook her head.

"Look at me." He waited for her until their gazes met. "I'm telling you this for your own good."

Something akin to pain flared in her eyes.

"There's no way we can convince David Rico that I'm your girlfriend. We aren't exactly…"

"I think we can be quite convincing." He brushed her bottom lip with the pad of his thumb. "I'm willing to start over, if you are."

Delaney stared at him as if to gauge his sincerity.

For a moment, Jack thought she wasn't going to respond. He wasn't sure what he'd do, if she didn't.

Finally she nodded. "I can do that."

"Fair enough." It wasn't quite the answer Jack had been hoping for, but it was a start. "I don't think you have to worry about convincing Rico."

"Why?"

"You had me convinced you were a flight attendant."

She huffed. "That's different. I trained for that position. Technically, I'm qualified to work for the airline as a flight attendant."

Jack threw his head back and laughed. "You actually went through training?"

"Yes, why?"

"Because, honey, you are the worst flight attendant I've ever seen."

"I wasn't that bad," Delaney retorted.

"Like hell you weren't. Every time the plane hit an air pocket your cheeks drained of color and you clung to the seat belt. You're so scared of flying. Aren't you?"

Delaney swallowed hard and she glanced at her feet. She looked everywhere but at him.

"It's okay. Everyone is scared of something." Jack brushed her cheek with the back of his hand.

"What are you frightened of?" she asked.

Loss of his freedom, he thought, before answering, "Nothing."

"Yeah, right." She glared at him, but he could tell she was trying not to smile. "You just told me that everyone is afraid of something. Don't make me punch you and ruin that handsome face."

His grin kicked up a notch. "You think I'm handsome?"

"Oh, please, a corpse would find you good-looking."

"Thanks, I think," he said, sobering at the mention of a corpse. "We'll have to do a helluva job making sure Rico believes we're a couple. He's been known to stake out potential business associates. Not that I anticipate him going that far, but you never know. If he has the slightest doubts that we're not who we say we are, he'll make us wish we were never born."

Delaney blew out a heavy breath. "What exactly does that mean? Keep in mind, we only have a few days to make contact and get the information. And that's if we're lucky. If he doesn't know anything, this case is going to fall apart and a lot of innocent people are going to die."

"I mean if you want to pull this off we're going to have to

stay in character at all times. Last night was a good place to start, but from here on out we'll have to eat together, live together, bathe together and sleep together. You must be willing to do whatever I ask. Rico can't suspect that you don't do everything I tell you to do." His lips canted in amusement.

JACK HAD LOST his ever-loving mind if he thought that she would do everything a man told her to. Her mother had spent her whole life fulfilling the role of the perfect wife, never raising her voice, always being an exemplary hostess. Delaney still didn't understand how her mother had given up her dreams of becoming a nurse so easily in order to appease a man. She was nothing like her mother.

Delaney recalled the evening prior. She may have bowed down before the "altar of Jack" a couple of times last night. It hadn't been too difficult and it certainly wasn't unpleasant. If she were honest with herself, Delaney could admit she actually enjoyed it, but that wasn't the same as what her mother had done. Or so she preferred to believe.

Could she pretend to be Jack's? Sleep in his bed, stay in his home, and spend all her time with him? Those questions did strange fluttery things to her insides. She'd only been prepared for one night of hot sex, not multiple evenings. Continuous close contact would create emotional complications she didn't need or want, but what choice did she have?

Delaney wanted to stop this shipment and close this case. It wasn't as if there was anything else going on between her and Jack…beyond sex. This was an assignment. He was an assignment. Despite falling into bed with him, Delaney wasn't altogether sure she could trust him.

What if he sold her out to David Rico? Would he do that after warning her? She shuddered at the thought. The truth was she didn't know Jack Gordon other than biblically.

"I think you're enjoying this turn of events a little too much, but I'll see what my group supervisor has to say," Delaney offered.

"You do that." His amused tone grated on her nerves.

"He may scrap this whole plan. You understand that, right?" she challenged, thinking McMillan would probably give her the go-ahead after he ripped her a new one for blowing cover. She underestimated Jack once, while searching his office, but she'd never do it again.

The statement brought a smile to his face. He didn't have to look so damn happy about it. If she didn't know any better, Delaney would swear Jack knew that wasn't going to happen.

He gripped her hip as he brushed past. The warmth from his touch seared her flesh, sending heat branching out in all directions. He walked over to the bed and grabbed her purse. *What was he up to?* she wondered.

He reached into it without permission and took out her USB drive. *How did he know?* He tossed the drive into the air and caught it, before pitching the purse to Delaney. She caught it without thinking, her fist closing around the strap.

"I think I'll keep this if you don't mind, since what's on it is my property. That is unless you have a search warrant tucked somewhere else." Jack had the audacity to lean forward to look down her blouse. There was a flash of dimple in his cheek and his blue eyes sparkled with mirth as he held back a laugh. "I'll see you back here this evening." He glanced at the clock next to his bed. "Say six? I expect an answer then."

Delaney tossed the strap of her purse over her shoulder. "You're pretty sure of yourself."

"Always," he said, guiding her out of the bedroom. With his hand resting on the small of her back he walked her to her car.

She glanced at his hands, which rested on her door. Those

fingers had played her body like a harp, soft when she needed soft and firm when she needed to be pushed over the edge.

"It's not too late to call this off."

The concern in Jack's voice was unmistakable. The protectiveness he displayed wreaked havoc with Delaney's emotions. What was the matter with him? He should hate her for what she'd done to him. If their roles were reversed, goodness knows she would.

His caring only added to her confusion. No one outside of her family had ever shown this much concern for her well-being. Against her wishes, Delaney's heart swelled. Unfortunately, that burst of emotion didn't change what she had to do. "You know I can't call off this mission."

"Yes, but I need to know something before you leave," he said.

"What?"

Jack shaded his eyes from the sun. His expression changed as he peered down at her. "Do you think I'm one of the bad guys?"

She didn't know how to answer. She'd certainly considered him bad, even if he hadn't been caught breaking the law. And what if he turned out to be responsible for what happened to Elaine? No one should be shot while they're trying to help others. What would she do then? Delaney wasn't sure what to think now. Sleeping with Jack had been a huge mistake. The newly developed intimacy was clouding her judgment. In the end, she decided to be diplomatic—at least until she found out the truth.

"The jury is still undecided."

He released a frustrated breath as his blue gaze probed her face. Eventually he spoke. "Okay...for now." He paused. "If we're to convince Rico we're a couple, then we'll need all the practice we can get. See you tonight."

How had things gotten so screwed up? She'd been on a few undercover operations. Granted, none were particularly important or nearly as dangerous as this mission, but she wasn't a rookie. Yet, somehow Jack had managed to lift the case out of her hands and take over. McMillan would surely lose it completely, that is if he didn't fire her first.

Jack shut the door as she started her engine. She needed to go home, get away from this man and clear her head. She also needed a shower before she drove in to the office. She smelled like Jack and sex, not exactly ATF presentable.

Delaney groaned, staring at Jack in her rearview mirror as she wound her way down his drive. He raised a hand and waved before turning back to his front door. Delaney didn't stop watching until he'd disappeared inside. She was in over her head with this one and the fallout wasn't going to be pretty.

"YOU DID WHAT?" McMillan bellowed, walking around his desk and slamming the door on the shocked faces of the office staff.

"I agreed to let Jack take the lead with Rico. He says he doesn't know who's behind the deal, but he thinks Rico could be connected. Like everything else in this case, it's a long shot. Jack said he'll use his boat to lure Rico into a meet."

McMillan sat back down. "That's what I thought you said. Anderson is going to pop a gasket when I tell him. You realize that he'll insist on overseeing the case from here on out, don't you?" McMillan reached into his desk and pulled out a bottle of aspirin. He thumbed the lid off and popped two tablets into his mouth, then chewed, not bothering with water.

Delaney's mouth went bone-dry as she watched. She rubbed her tongue over the roof of her mouth and swallowed hard. "I didn't have much choice. It was either that or he was going to walk."

McMillan's brows drew down. "Do you think he's telling the truth?"

Delaney froze. Did she think Jack was telling the truth?

Yes, oddly enough. With his dislike of David Rico, she couldn't think of a reason for him to lie. "I believe Jack's being straight with me. I mean us," she said, displaying a level of trust she didn't know she was capable of.

"You don't have the authority to make those kinds of calls, period. I ought to bust you back down to GS-5 and that's just for starters."

She flinched. "Yes, sir, but this was a special circumstance."

His eyes narrowed. "Does that special circumstance have anything to do with this?" McMillan spun his laptop around until she could see the screen. A blurry image of she and Jack kissing—naked—stared back at her.

Delaney felt her face pale and her stomach drop. "You filmed us." Her voice cracked. She'd be a laughingstock if that recording was leaked to the rest of the Bureau. If? She silently groaned. More like when. She wondered how many copies were already in circulation.

McMillan looked disappointed. "I couldn't exactly send you in there without backup. Besides, I didn't give the order. Anderson did."

"You could've told me. Warned me that they'd be out there."

"I would've, if I'd had any idea this would happen." He pressed a button and the image disappeared.

It took Delaney a moment to pull herself together. "We needed Jack's cooperation. That's why I went through flight attendant training, why the Bureau placed me on his flights, and why I'm here before you now. You said to get Jack's cooperation any way I could. Well, I did."

"I know what I said. That does not change the fact that you slept with this man and gave him classified information. What were you thinking? Must I remind you of protocol?"

"It couldn't be avoided. Jack was already suspicious after he caught me coming out of his office this morning. He gave me an ultimatum. I did what was best for the case. It was strictly a business decision."

McMillan stared at her intently. Slowly he asked, "What's really going on here, Delaney? You know I think of you like a second daughter."

"I know, sir," she said, wincing at his admission.

"This could cost you your promotion. Your job. This is so out of character for you that I have to ask. Do you care for this man?"

Delaney felt heat rise, engulf her ears, then radiate out through the top of her head. "No," she croaked. "I don't care about him." Her heart clenched in protest. "How could you ask such a thing?"

"It's not only me who wants to know. Anderson specifically phoned to find out what you uncovered."

"Great." She sighed.

McMillan's shoulders relaxed. "It isn't a problem if you do care for him. As far as we can tell, Jack Gordon's still clean. I haven't found a connection yet that would tie him to Elaine. He appears to be legit, unless you've uncovered new evidence to the contrary."

Her mind instantly flashed to the plane and Jack's carry-on luggage. "I—I..." she stuttered, then her shoulders slumped. "No."

"I didn't think so. That news disappointed the hell out of Anderson, but what doesn't these days?" He chortled, then quickly sobered. "You'll have to be on top of your game. You cannot be distracted. Tell me now whether you think we can proceed as scheduled."

"I believe we can. Do you want me to notify the airline or would you like to?"

"Notify the airline?" he asked, clearly confused.

"Since Jack already knows who I am, I didn't think there was a reason to continue with the charade."

"You'll stay undercover until this case is over. Understand?"

"Yes, sir."

McMillan closed his eyes and scrubbed his beefy hands over his shaven face. "Your father will never forgive me for this one, especially if anything happens to you. He's already had one daughter injured. I don't think he could handle another. Here, I thought I was doing him a favor, as one war buddy to another."

"It has nothing to do with my past," she lied. Delaney stiffened at the mention of her dad. "And nothing to do with my father, either. I made my own decisions." Things had gotten out of hand momentarily, but now the assignment was back on track. That was all that was important.

He frowned, then made a few calls, leaving her to wrestle with her thoughts.

"Against my better judgment, Special-Agent-in-Charge Anderson has agreed to meet Gordon's demands. He's hoping that if we give Jack enough rope, he'll hang himself," he said, putting down the phone receiver.

Delaney steeled her expression so McMillan couldn't see how much his words were affecting her.

"I hope you know what you're doing. At sea would be a hell of a time to find out that you were wrong about Gordon. We won't be able to watch you aboard his boat. Rico would spot a helicopter hovering around. We'll have a boat on standby, but it won't be close by. If anything happened, we would be too late to save you." He sat in silence, letting his last statement sink in.

"I understand, but I think we'll have to take a chance and trust Jack." And they weren't the only ones. She was, too. "I'm not sure what he's up to financially. There are still a few questions I need answered, but I don't think they'll come until after the shipment arrives."

"And?"

"I can see no way to proceed until I meet with Rico and see if he knows anything about the incoming weapons. We're down to the wire, chief and you know it. I know we're taking a big chance by contacting Rico without definitive intel that he has the information that we need, but what choice do we have?"

"I still don't like it," McMillan grumbled.

Delaney rose, then took a shaky breath before she answered. "I'm aware of that, sir. The plan is far from ideal, but with the deadline we're working against, I see no other option."

"You cannot get emotionally entangled—until this case closes."

She tensed. "I'm not. It was a temporary lack of judgment and it won't happen again."

His brow rose. Without a word, McMillan flicked a button to bring up the frozen picture of Jack and Delaney on the video screen. "Lack of judgment? Is that what you call what you're doing here?"

"No." Her jaw clenched. "I call that doing my job, sir."

9

JACK SLIPPED THE KEY into the front door of his house. It had been a long afternoon, but he'd managed to successfully place part of his art collection with the famous Heard Museum in downtown Phoenix. He crossed the threshold and went directly to punch in the code to the silent alarm.

As his fingers neared the pad, he noticed it was disarmed. Jack tensed, and his hand slipped fluidly to the small of his back where he grasped the handle of his Glock. He was about to pull the weapon when a familiar feminine voice called out.

"Rough day at the office, dear."

Jack's muscles eased and he released his gun, then turned to face Delaney. She was lounging barefoot on his couch with a magazine propped on her stomach, looking like the Queen of Sheba. Her sweet brown eyes sparkled with mischief. Jack decided she was the most adorable thing he'd ever seen. He clamped down on the urge to cross the room and pull her into his arms. Instead, he glanced at his watch. "You're early. I didn't expect you until this evening."

"What can I say? I couldn't stand to be away from you that long."

He snorted. "I bet. How did you get past my security?"

"You'd be amazed at what I've learned how to do over the years."

"Oh, really?" He reached into his pocket, plucking his cell phone out, and began to dial.

"Who are you phoning?"

"My security company."

Delaney frowned. "Why?"

Jack smiled, but didn't answer her. "This is Mr. Gordon. Starting next week, your services will no longer be needed." He pressed a button, disconnecting the call.

Her mouth dropped open. "Why did you fire them?"

He laughed. "Because they aren't doing the job I paid them for. Can I get you something to drink?"

"Sure."

"White or red?" he asked, heading to the minibar.

"Red."

Jack returned carrying two glasses of wine and handed one to Delaney. She'd pulled her brown hair back, leaving her face and soft eyes visible. He longed to touch her, but first he wanted to find out why she was here. There was something different about her, a newfound confidence that he hadn't detected before. The duality of her nature made him slightly uneasy. Had she been able to meet his demands? He almost hoped not. He didn't want Delaney to get hurt.

"What did your boss say?" he asked, raising the glass to his lips. The wine burned as he swallowed. Delaney mirrored his actions, wetting her lips with the garnet liquid. Jack wanted so bad to lick the lingering moisture off. He took a step back to put some distance between them.

Delaney smiled knowingly. "He's agreed to meet your terms if you can get us in contact with David Rico."

"I put out the word to my friends in California that I was looking for a buyer for my boat. I made sure that they'd contact Rico's people. Did you get the word out about me doing a deal?"

She set the wineglass down on the coffee table. "I personally sent out the information before I left the office."

"How long do you think it'll take to reach L.A.?" he asked, sitting in his overstuffed chair.

"With the Internet, not long."

Jack nodded. It sounded as if they'd covered all their bases could for now. All that was left to do was wait and see if Rico took the bait. Jack's gaze drank in Delaney, from her small painted toes to her lovely rich hair. "Have you eaten?" he asked, suddenly famished.

She shook her head. "I can't stay long."

He frowned. "What do you mean you can't stay? I thought we agreed that you'd play the role of my girlfriend until this assignment ended."

She laughed. "I did, but since Rico hasn't contacted you, I doubt very much he'll be watching tonight." She had him and she knew it.

"And your point is?"

Delaney grinned mischievously. "That there's no need for me to spend the night."

Jack rose before he knew what he was doing. He crossed the distance separating them and grabbed Delaney by the upper arms, pulling her to her feet. The second her toes touched the ground, his lips were on her. Heat seared his gut as he devoured her mouth, coaxing her to open for him. Delaney didn't disappoint. Their tongues clashed, battling and twisting like a serpent mating dance.

His hands fisted her shirt, wanting—no, needing—to get closer. Delaney stopped him before he could remove it. He tore his mouth away, his breath staggering in his chest. "I want you so bad."

DELANEY WANTED HIM, too, but she wouldn't allow herself to get caught up in the moment again. The last time had landed her on video. She'd come here to tell him what McMillan had agreed upon and planned to leave right afterward. She needed to get home and pack in case Rico called and they had to catch a flight out to L.A.

"I can't stay," she repeated, trying to get her feet to cooperate.

Jack licked his bottom lip as if savoring her taste. The hard ridge of his erection pressed into her. His blue gaze swept her with such heat and hunger it almost took her breath away.

"If you're done torturing me, the least you can do is stay for dinner."

Delaney opened her mouth to answer when the phone rang.

"Excuse me," Jack said, then reached for his cell.

Delaney picked up her wine. She thought to leave the room to give Jack some privacy, but realized who was on the other line.

"Sure, I can meet him there tomorrow at..." He glanced at Delaney.

She shrugged, then mouthed eleven thirty.

"Eleven thirty," Jack relayed to the caller. "Good, I'll be there." He disconnected.

"That was David Rico, wasn't it?" she asked, approaching.

Jack shook his head. "No, it was his people. Rico doesn't make personal phone calls unless he deems them important."

"I guess buying a boat doesn't exactly fall in that category."

Jack smiled. "No, it doesn't." He brushed his fingers over her face.

"So we're meeting him tomorrow? Where?" she asked, knowing she'd have to phone McMillan and fill him in on the latest. She also needed to pack, since they'd be going back to California.

"My boat's docked at Marina Del Rey. We'll have to catch

a flight to Los Angeles first thing in the morning." He stepped closer. "You could always spend the night so we could practice the whole boyfriend-girlfriend thing."

"As tempting as that is, I'd better go."

"I thought we'd agreed upon dinner," he said, sounding decidedly put out.

"Actually, I don't remember agreeing to anything." Delaney reached up and kissed him on the chin. "See you in the morning Jack. Sleep tight."

She heard grumbles as she reached the heavy wooden door, then a very clear voice said, "You won't get away so easily tomorrow." Delaney hid her smile and stepped out into the warm desert air.

DELANEY STOOD as the plane leveled out. She wanted to grab drinks before Jeremy started his service. It felt wrong to make him wait on her and Jack. Her heart bounced with each air pocket. Nothing in the world could convince her that this mode of transportation was safe. Screw the statistics.

Jack sat in his first-class seat, watching her every move. His "I'm here for you if you need me" expression did strange things to her insides while lending her quiet strength. She gave him one last look before she stepped into the galley.

She hadn't slept much the previous night thanks to thoughts of Jack and the upcoming meet with David Rico.

"I see you're traveling with Mr. Yummy," Jeremy said from beside her.

Delaney glanced over her shoulder and shot him a look that she hoped said "back off." She was tired and she hadn't had her daily rationing of coffee yet.

"Don't shoot that attitude at me, girlfriend. I'm not the one who stayed up having monkey sex last night. Although I wish I had."

"We didn't have monkey sex...last night."

"But you did sleep with him."

She blushed. "How did you know?"

He grinned. "You just admitted it. Besides, Mr. Yummy hasn't taken his eyes off you since you boarded the plane." Jeremy inched closer. "Tell me, is he as good as he looks?"

"A girl never tells."

"Oh, please, you know I have to live vicariously through you, since you won't let me touch."

She laughed. "You're unbelievable."

"So I've been told." He pretended to buff his nails on his shirt. "Now come on. Do tell. I'd share the details if I'd rolled him in the sack."

Delaney glanced around the galley wall in Jack's direction. He winked at her.

Jeremy cleared his throat to remind her that he was still there.

Delaney started, then turned to beam at him. "He's better."

"Oh, girl, I knew it," he said with dramatic flair, then sauntered off, repeating "I knew it" under his breath.

She grabbed the two cups of coffee she'd poured and returned to her seat.

THE PLANE TOUCHED DOWN right on time. Delaney reached for her suitcase, but Jack got there first. "I'll get these and wait for you at the top of the jetway," he said, nodding toward Jeremy and Barbie, who were motioning to Delaney. A third flight attendant she'd never seen before brought up the rear.

"Thanks," she said.

The flight attendants pulled their bags behind them, making their way up the aisle.

Jeremy stopped when he reached her. "Even though you didn't work this one with us, I just love flying with you. Your trips are much shorter. The company must be trying something new with the probies. When I started, they flew us like dogs."

"Yeah, well, don't get used to the minimized schedule, Romeo. I'm not sure I'm cut out for this job."

He made a face. "It takes a while, but once you do, the job's not so bad."

"I don't know," Delaney said, shaking her head.

"Is it us? Sometimes the training flight attendants can be rough on the newbies. We've tried to lighten your load."

Delaney laughed. "It's not you guys, if anything I've been difficult." She wanted so bad to tell them the truth. They deserved that much, but she couldn't. Not yet anyway. "Well, I'd better scoot. Mr. Yummy is waiting." She winked at Jeremy.

"Sure, rub it in."

Jack took quick glances at his watch. "We don't have much time," he said, wheeling the bags expertly through Los Angeles International Airport. "We'll have to go straight there from here."

"Shouldn't I change clothes?" she asked, glancing down at her jeans.

"It would be better if you were in your uniform, but it really doesn't matter. I can always tell him that you're a stewardess."

"Flight attendant," she corrected without thought.

He looked over his shoulder. "My apologies, flight attendant."

Delaney glared mockingly. Jack didn't look sorry. He never looked sorry. She kicked the back of her bag and his footsteps faltered. He narrowed his eyes and grinned. Delaney looked at the wall as if nothing happened. Immature, yes, but it made her feel better.

"I'll get you back later." The promise in his voice turned her to mush. They were about to face someone who possibly held the key to a potential threat to the nation's security and here she was flirting.

She'd gone from rigidly detached while on the job to neck-deep involvement. The agents she'd worked with in the past would be shocked that the Ice Queen had finally melted.

Jack rented a car at the airport and drove in silence to Marina Del Rey, a quiet suburb of Los Angeles. Homes ranging from 1960s bungalows to modern architectural show pieces lined the beach in a hiccup fashion, all trying to capitalize on the stunning Pacific Ocean views.

A paved walkway split the sandy beach like an unruly hair part, giving the residents and visitors a place to partake in outdoor recreation year-round. Delaney watched as two people on Rollerblades barely missed a man walking his Pomeranian.

Jack's boat was parked in one of the far slips of a substantial marina. Delaney followed him down the wood planked dock, keeping an eye on her surroundings. It wasn't that she didn't trust Jack—she did, but the lack of backup made her nervous. To make matters worse, she couldn't bring her gun, which meant she had to rely on Jack and her own quick thinking if things went south.

"Here she is," Jack said, turning to grin at Delaney.

She looked at his craft and gaped. "This is your modest-sized boat?"

"I never lie about size." He chuckled wagging his eyebrows. "Besides, forty-three feet is modest in certain circles."

Delaney was agog. Boys and their toys. No wonder David Rico was interested in Jack's boat. It was magnificent in a completely over-the-top way and obviously made for gliding across the waves. "How fast does it go?" she asked.

"A Scarab can reach over eighty miles an hour."

She stared at the boat, then at the ocean's calm waters. At

eighty miles an hour, the hull would be like a rock skipping over the surface. "What time is Rico due here?" she asked, nervously.

Jack's expression sobered. "I told him to meet us." He glanced at his watch. "In about thirty minutes."

"At least we have some time to mentally and physically prepare," she said.

"Let's hope we don't need it."

10

DAVID RICO ARRIVED at the dock at eleven thirty sharp in his black Escalade. Dressed casually in expensive black trousers and a light sweater, he looked more like a college student than an arms dealer. His blondish-brown hair was spiked in the latest style and appeared to match his designer sunglasses.

Although less than physically impressive, he walked with a confidence that came from possessing power. Behind him, two men in dark Armani suits and sunglasses followed at a respectable distance. Their gazes scanned the surrounding boats, taking in every detail down to the last squawking seagull. Delaney half expected them to reach into their jackets to rest their hands on the firearms their suits didn't quite conceal.

Her lips thinned as she glanced at Jack, who met her eyes with calm reassurance. He stepped forward to greet David Rico, his hand extended.

"Mr. Rico, thank you for calling about the boat. I know how busy you are these days, so I won't take up too much of your time." Rico removed his sunglasses and looked at Jack's hand, then at the two bruisers behind him. The men stepped forward and frisked Jack.

When the men finished, they turned as one to David Rico. "He's clean," the shorter of the two said, then moved on to Delaney.

"Hey, what's the deal?" she asked, swatting the guy's

meaty hand away from the wraparound skirt she'd used to conceal her bathing suit. Delaney glowered at Jack and hoped Rico believed her performance. "Honey, why is this man touching me?"

Jack didn't acknowledge her question.

"She's clean, too," the man said, smirking before stepping away.

"Now, sweetheart, I told you not to speak unless you were spoken to," Jack admonished, sending her a warning glare.

"Sorry," she apologized quickly.

He turned to David Rico. "Women," he said as if that explained everything.

David Rico glanced between them and laughed. He extended his hand to Jack. "It's nice to finally meet you, Jack Gordon. I've heard so much about you, including your recent escapades on the east coast."

"I like to stay busy."

"Is that so? I'll have to keep that in mind."

Jack grinned, his normal warmth replaced by cool calculation. "Please come aboard."

Rico nodded at his men and they boarded the craft first to search the boat. A few minutes later, they gave the all-clear signal and he climbed aboard.

The shorter bodyguard kept sneaking covert glances at Delaney. She wasn't sure if it was due to his suspicions, or the fact that he'd nearly felt her up during the weapons search. Sparky could keep his hands to himself or she'd break them.

Jack and Rico settled in at the front of the boat, while the two bodyguards and Delaney were relegated to the rear.

Delaney tried to hear what was being said, but it was useless against the *thub, thub* of the motors behind her. Jack pointed to various items near the steering column and appeared to be going over the boat's selling points. She hoped he eventually got around to asking about the shipment. Although how he'd work it into the conversation she didn't know.

Maybe David Rico was too low in the ranks like McMillan said and he didn't have any useful information. Her heart sank. There was no sense guessing the next move, until they found out for sure. She'd hate to think they went to all this trouble for nothing. Delaney shivered as the boat backed out of the slip and headed out to sea.

They'd been going at a steady clip when Jack suddenly opened up the boat on the water. Wind whipped the occupants as the Scarab flew across the waves.

David Rico laughed at something Jack said, then tossed a glance back at them. His gaze lingered on Delaney longer than she'd have liked. It wasn't hunger she saw in his gray depths, but the promise of death. His appraisal was cold and calculating—he was the exact opposite of Jack.

What if Jack did sell her out? The thought scared her almost as much as Rico's gaze did. She scanned the shore, attempting to gauge her chances of surviving the long swim. They were dismal at best, since her strongest stroke was a dog paddle. Rico turned back to Jack and thumped him on the shoulder.

He leaned in and said something, which had Jack turning to look at her. He grinned, but the smile did not reach his lovely blue eyes. Delaney shuddered. She couldn't help it. She didn't like being kept out of the loop.

How well did she really know Jack, anyway? So they'd had sex and enjoyed a few meals. That didn't mean anything. Delaney knew she was overreacting and that everything was happening as planned.

Jack and Rico switched places smoothly despite the boat's bouncing as it hit the waves. He made his way back to where she sat and then leaned down to kiss her, his hand moving casually to her hip. David Rico leered at the exchange. This wasn't anything like she'd imagined her assignment to be—it was worse.

Delaney wanted to arrest every last one of them, but McMillan was counting on her. For that reason alone, she allowed Jack to fondle her as if she were a piece of sky fluff. She supposed to men like Rico, who thought women were possessions, she was a toy. Much like the boat. Delaney nipped Jack's lip and saw his eyes widen.

"I didn't realize you liked it rough," he said, releasing her long enough to pull her to her feet.

Delaney gasped, trying to keep her balance. "That's not why I bit you."

"I know." Jack grinned, clearly enjoying their predicament way more than he should. "Be careful, you're playing with fire," he said, his mouth moving to her cheek. He kissed his way to her ear, nuzzling her neck. "I think we about have him."

"He's still watching us like he's afraid to miss part of the show," she whispered in his ear. "The guy is a deviant."

Jack shrugged. "Rico likes to watch. Why do you think he has his goons follow potential business partners with video surveillance equipment? He tends to mix his paranoia with a little kink. Let's not disappoint him."

"Are you suggesting what I think you're suggesting?" she asked under her breath.

"You're supposed to be my girlfriend, remember?" He nibbled her flesh, his hand stroking her back, soothingly. "It won't be much longer. Rico's interested in the boat and has said if we can agree on a price, then there may be more business opportunities in the future. He hasn't gone into details yet because that's not his style. Just play along if he invites you to join us in the conversation, but remember not to speak. In fact, it would be best if you act like you don't understand what we're talking about."

"Best or safest?" she asked.

"Both." Jack winked.

Delaney cursed softly, so only Jack could hear. He pulled back from her. "I had no idea you knew those dirty words. What other secrets have you been keeping from me?" Desire sparked in his eyes for a moment, then he kissed her one last time, long enough to whirl her senses, before returning to the seat beside Rico.

JACK GLANCED AT the man seated next to him. Rico looked like any other Californian: he was tanned, had bleached teeth and a trim body. It was only when you took a closer look that you noted the steel in his gray gaze, the almost imperceptible cold that seemed to emanate from him. It was as if Jack Frost had taken permanent refuge in his soul.

His interest in Delaney was clearly showing in his mercury eyes. Jack didn't like the look he was giving her and had the sudden urge to punch the guy in the nose. That, of course, would get him killed, but it was almost worth seeing the expression on Rico's smug face when it happened.

The bastard had a reputation for being ruthless and now Jack could see why. David Rico may wear the cloak of civility while he was in public, but the mask slipped often enough to glimpse the true man. Jack didn't like what he witnessed. The sooner they found out whether or not Rico had the information they needed, and got away from him, the better.

"So, do you think there's a chance I could spend some time with your lady friend?" Rico asked, shifting toward Jack with a sly grin.

Jack forced himself to remain expressionless. He didn't want Rico knowing that he actually cared for Delaney, but at the same time, he didn't want the guy thinking that he could have free reign with no repercussions.

"I'm grooming her to do a job for me," Jack said casually. "Why else would I date her?"

Rico's gaze stayed similarly neutral, but Jack noted his sudden interest. "What kind of job?" Rico asked, as he maneuvered the boat around, sending ocean spray over his bodyguards' heads.

They glared at him, then quickly looked away as if remembering their place. They wiped the water off their sunglasses and suit jackets. Jack grinned, happy to see water dripping off the face of the man who'd patted Delaney down. Maybe that would cool his jets.

Jack turned back to Rico. He had his full attention. It was now or never. He had to take a chance and play his hand to see just how involved Rico was in the business. Otherwise, they'd never get the matter sorted and Delaney would continue to needlessly endanger herself.

"She's a flight attendant for Moran South Air and has family connections on the ground in Phoenix that could get a shipment transported without anyone being the wiser," he said, making it up as he went. He sure hoped that the ATF would be able to supply whatever he created, if the time came.

"You don't say." Rico stared at Delaney once more. His sexual interest seemed to intensify.

Despite the churning in his stomach, Jack knew in that moment that they'd hooked him. He decided to reel Rico in to ensure he'd truly taken the bait. "I was thinking about testing her with a dummy shipment. See if she's as good a mule as I think."

Rico appeared to consider his words. "So you don't have anything specific set up yet?"

"No, I've had to lie low due to some unexpected heat from the ATF lately."

Rico snorted. "Yeah, they can be a real pain in the ass sometimes."

"Yeah, a pain." Jack glanced at Delaney.

"Luckily, I've found a way around them," Rico added.

Jack wanted to ask how, but he knew better. He looked straight ahead, watching the rise and fall of the bow of the boat as it skimmed across the water. "What do you think of the boat?" he asked.

"You know I love it. Are you going to sell it to me?"

Jack's lips quirked. "I haven't decided."

"Well, maybe I can do something for you that will sweeten the pot."

Jack's brow arched. "I'm all ears."

"I may know of a shipment coming in that needs to leave California quickly."

Jack faced him. "Is that so? What does that have to do with me?"

Rico dropped the speed of the boat, so it was easier to handle. "Tony, come up here and take the wheel. Mr. Gordon and I need to talk somewhere more private."

The beefy bodyguard rose and teetered toward the wheel. "I'm not sure how to drive a boat, boss."

"You can drive a car, can't you?" he asked, his voice becoming deadly.

"Yes, sir."

"This is the same idea." He let go of the wheel and stepped down into the cabin. "Make sure you don't hit anything. I want my boat in pristine condition."

"You got it, boss."

"Come with me," Rico said to Jack.

Delaney started to rise, but Jack stopped her with a quick jerk of his head.

He followed Rico into the cabin past the small wet bar and fridge to the bench seating. "Can I get you anything to drink?" Jack asked, opening the fridge and retrieving a beer.

"I'll take one of those," Rico said, making himself comfortable, as if he owned the place.

Jack handed him the drink, then sat across from him. "You said you wanted to talk, so talk," he said, trying to balance impatience with interest.

He wondered what was happening on deck. Were the bodyguards hassling Delaney? Logically, Jack knew she could take care of herself, but that knowledge didn't prevent the fear from seeping into his gut.

"I like you, Jack. You seem like the kind of guy who knows a good deal when he hears one," Rico said carefully, watching for a reaction to his words.

"Get to the point, David. I have a warm and willing woman on deck waiting for me to give her the word to come down here for a little playtime." He shifted, glancing at the door they'd just slipped through.

"Down, boy." David Rico laughed. "Women are great, aren't they? Especially once you show them who's boss. I could see by the way you were handling...what did you say her name was?"

"I didn't," Jack said coolly.

"Fine, names aren't important with chicks. I'm not interested in the end that speaks anyway. So tell me, is she as good as she looks? I picture her as a screamer. Am I right?" Rico asked, scooting to the edge of the cushioned bench and leaning in.

"She's better," Jack said, refusing to elaborate. He hated the feeling of betrayal that ripped through him. He didn't talk about bed sport and he certainly didn't discuss his lovers. Jack had more respect for the women he was with than to do that.

Then there was Delaney...

He wasn't quite sure where she fit in to his life. All Jack knew was that she felt special, different. She wasn't just another notch in his bed to be flaunted. He didn't want Rico or any other man cheapening what they'd shared over the past couple of days, regardless of what had brought them together.

Rico raised his bottle in mock salute. "I knew it, man. You could just tell by the way she looked at you."

"Looked at me? Looked at me how?" Jack frowned. What was Rico talking about?

"She looked like a woman in love."

"Love?" he choked on the word a second before warmth blossomed inside him.

"Well, if not love, then something damn close to it. If I'm right, then you've got it made. Women that care will do anything for their man, even go to prison for you. Believe me, I know. There's a chick I used to bang serving five to seven years as we speak." Rico's voice rose in excitement. "This could work out better than I imagined."

Jack was stunned. He couldn't seem to form a single thought. Was David Rico right? Was Delaney in love with him? Was that even possible given their short time together?

Normally, the thought of a woman falling in love with him would horrify Jack, but for some reason with Delaney it didn't. There was no panicky feeling like he'd experienced in the past, only a strange kind of calm. He couldn't decide what he felt. It was all a jumble in his mind. He'd have to examine it more closely later…if he lived through this meeting.

He blinked, coming out of his haze when he realized Rico was still talking.

"There is something about that innocent girl-next-door thing she has going on that just screams 'fuck me.' Sure you won't share?"

The man couldn't be serious. Jack stared at him. Not a flicker of doubt showed in Rico's tanned face.

"Positive," Jack said, tilting his beer bottle in minisalute.

He'd met plenty of guys like David Rico when he'd been in the business. Most were up-and-comers with no talent and even fewer brains. They tended to die early or quit, if they were lucky. Most weren't lucky. Unfortunately, Rico was the real deal. He had intelligence, albeit hidden, and talent to go with a healthy dose of driving ambition and devout viciousness.

"So tell me more about this possible deal," Jack said, changing tack.

"Like I said, I may know of a shipment, containing RPG Grenades, AK-47s, ammo, the ingredients for a few dirty bombs, and five hundred pounds of C4 that needs transport to a more central location. See, I have a little auction lined up. Nothing big. Half a dozen buyers max. These are very important people who've been looking forward to this gathering for some time. I wouldn't want to disappoint them. It's bad for business. Do you think you and your honey could handle something like that?"

Jack took a swig of beer, pretending to contemplate his offer. "I think we could manage. Her family owns a van rental agency near the Phoenix airport. We could borrow as many as we needed to come here to L.A. and pick up the merchandise. Of course, it may take a few days to arrange everything."

David Rico's expression darkened. "I need five vans and you'd have two."

"Two days? That's awful quick, don't you think? I haven't even talked to my lady yet." Did the ATF have it together enough to move that quickly? Would Delaney be ready? The thought of anything happening to her tightened Jack's chest to the point he could hardly breathe. He exhaled.

"The auction date is already set. The buyers are not going to wait for you to get it together. Either you can handle this job or you can't." Rico's eyes went cold. "Are you worried that you can't control your woman? I can speak to her if that's a concern."

"That won't be necessary. She'll do exactly what I say without question."

Rico considered him for a moment. "I'm only going to make this offer once." He sat back on the cushions, picking the label off the outside of the beer bottle. "What do you say?"

Jack took another swig of beer to steady his nerves. He hoped like hell that Delaney and her people were ready for this deal to go down. If not, he had no doubt David Rico would be less than forgiving when he found out that Jack didn't have any connections. He'd burned those bridges long ago.

"Where is the shipment being stored at present?" Jack asked.

"All you need to know is that it's safe," Rico said without answering the question.

"I think we need to know more than that, if you want us to pick it up."

"All in good time."

"Okay," he said, not liking that they were being kept from so many details. Jack held out his hand to shake. "I guess we've got a deal."

David Rico clamped down, threatening to crush bone, his gaze boring into Jack's. "I don't back out of deals, Jack. And I don't allow anyone else to, either."

Jack returned his grip, then tried to pull away, but the man held on. "What am I missing here?" he asked, twisting his wrist to break contact. Rico held on like a pit bull, strangely strong for such a small man.

"I like to know the people I do business with are as committed to the success of the job as I am." He leveled his gaze.

"We are. I give you my word." Jack tugged.

Rico gave him a shark's tooth grin. "I don't think you're hearing me, Jack."

"I hear you clearly. You want a commitment. Fine, I'll give it to you—after you give me some reassurance. I need something to convince the woman to take the risk."

"That's too bad, Jack." He stood, releasing him suddenly. "I was really looking forward to working with you, but I guess we're done here." Rico walked toward the stairs that led to the deck.

"Wait," Jack called out, knowing he was about to regret his next question. "What kind of commitment do you need?"

Rico turned, not bothering to hide the triumph on his face. "So glad you asked. Since I'm feeling magnanimous, I will give you a choice. You can either come to work for me, starting tonight at eight o'clock in the Queen Mary luxury liner parking lot in Long Beach." He gazed out the small porthole at the ocean, his irises dilating. "Or I get one night with your woman."

"Excuse me?" Jack's stomach lurched in panic.

Rico flashed him an easy smile that was anything but warm. "Simple. You get to earn money, let's say fifty large, or I get to taste that sexy piece of ass waiting for you on deck. Personally, I know which one I'd choose."

Jack couldn't exactly hand Delaney over to this animal, but he didn't like the idea of being forced into a job. He pictured Delaney on deck in her bikini, then glanced at Rico's smug expression. The bastard had him and they both knew it. Rico made an offer Jack couldn't refuse. He was damned if he did and damned if he didn't. He reached for his beer and downed the contents, then slammed the empty bottle onto the bench beside him.

"The woman is mine." He seethed at the way he'd been played by Rico. The man was good, he'd give him that.

"Oh, Jack, I'm disappointed." He tsked.

"Why?"

"Because I can get any idiot to do the job. I was really looking forward to a night with your girl." Rico shook his head. "Wouldn't have taken you for the sentimental type. She must really be something."

You'll never find out, Jack thought. He glared at Rico, allowing the anger and hatred he'd been concealing to show. "I don't care about the woman," he lied smoothly. "But I do care about the big job—and the money it'll bring. We need her to be in *perfect* condition in order to pull this off. She has to convince her family to allow her to use a quarter of their fleet without raising suspicion. What happens between you and her afterward is up to you." Jack shrugged nonchalantly, feeling anything but.

Rico started to sit back down, then stopped at the last second and straightened. "Glad to hear you say that, Jack. I can't wait to take a taste of that sweet mouth of hers."

The thought of David Rico touching Delaney brought a whole new level of violence out in Jack. Something primal and dangerous rose within him. He clenched his fists in impotent rage as his vision blurred to red. At that moment, Jack knew with absolute certainty that he'd kill the bastard before he'd allow that to happen.

11

WHAT WAS TAKING them so long? Delaney scanned the horizon, her nerves fraying at the ends. Were they still discussing the deal or had David Rico caught on to their scheme? She hadn't heard any arguing, but that didn't mean anything.

She looked at the burly bodyguards. The one driving the boat had a death grip on the wheel. He'd come close to hitting two other boats and a buoy in the last ten minutes. If Jack and Rico didn't come back soon, she was going to push Tony aside and drive them back to the marina.

She shook her head. There wasn't anything she could do other than get as much information as possible and hope that was enough to put Rico away somewhere down the line, so he'd never be able to operate again. Delaney could only hope Jack was getting what they needed.

Rico came out of the cabin a few minutes later. His gaze lingered on her body, taking in her legs and flat abdomen. The appraisal slithered over her senses like a python, right before it crushes its prey. Delaney fought the urge to retch. Rico smiled at her and then pushed Tony out of the way so that he could step behind the wheel.

Delaney's gaze bulleted to the cabin door. Where was Jack? Her heart raced as panic seized her. She didn't relax until she saw the top of his dark hair appear out of the shadows. Delaney sighed and some of the tension in her chest receded.

That was until she caught his expression. It was vacant. Empty, not anything like the typical Jack.

She tensed, preparing to dive overboard if the situation demanded it. Jack watched her, a myriad of emotions swirling in his blue depths. He nodded to Rico and then walked the few feet separating them and sat next to Delaney.

She wanted to ask how it went, but from the set of his jaw and the warning in his eyes, Delaney thought better of it. He didn't look happy. What had happened down there? Had Rico told them what they needed to know? Was Jack upset because he didn't have any information? The questions swirled in her mind until her head spun.

Rico whipped the boat around and headed back to the marina. He threw the engines into idle as they drew closer, signaling Jack to come forward and take over. The goons jumped on the dock and grabbed the tie ropes as Jack guided the boat into the slip. Rico slapped Jack on the back as he reached for the Scarab's keys.

"I'll take it," he said.

Delaney frowned, watching the exchange. Why had Jack handed over the keys to his boat? That hadn't been part of the deal. The boat was only to lure Rico here. Delaney knew she was missing something vital.

"It's been a pleasure doing business with you, Jack," he said, turning to Delaney. "I look forward to seeing more of you in the very near future."

Delaney didn't say anything. What could she say? She wasn't sure what Rico meant and couldn't exactly ask Jack. What she did know was that she didn't like the way Rico was looking at her. The impression of ownership was unmistakable.

She and Jack stood on the dock, watching Rico's retreating back. As soon as they were out of earshot, Delaney turned to Jack.

"You want to tell me what just happened? Why did you give that jerk the keys to your boat? You weren't actually supposed to sell it."

He threw her a glance, anger shimmering in his eyes. "I don't want to talk about it."

Something was definitely wrong. Her gut twisted, but she decided to take a different approach. She considered whether or not she should push Jack right now, he might withdraw completely. "Did Rico have any information about the deal?" she asked, undeterred by his mood.

"I said I don't want to talk about it."

"Jack." She touched his sleeve and met his turbulent gaze. "I need to know."

"He's behind the whole deal."

Delaney was stunned. She couldn't be that lucky to have found the main player. "All our intel on him says he's small-time. Are you serious?"

"Dead...serious."

McMillan would be thrilled. The news was so good that he may even forgive her for turning the case over to Jack and promote her.

"What did Rico say exactly?"

"He wants us to move the shipment for him. I told him your family owned a van rental agency in Phoenix and that we could borrow as many as was needed to transport the weapons. We'll have to get the vans and drive them here to L.A. so everything appears normal."

She nodded. "That's perfect. Now we have time to set everything up. Thank you, Jack."

He rubbed the back of his neck, the tension clear in his face. "Don't thank me so quickly. He wants this deal to go down in two days. He's apparently set up an auction for the buyers."

"Damn! I don't know if we can get things arranged that quickly."

"I thought your people had everything worked out." Jack smirked.

"What were you thinking?"

"I was thinking how much I enjoy breathing. I was also thinking that agreeing to do the job was the only way we were going to catch this bastard. It was either that or swim back to shore. That's what I was thinking." Anger bubbled out of Jack, scorching his words.

Delaney waited for him to finish. There was more going on here than mere negotiations. Jack still hadn't explained what had happened to his boat or why he was mad at her. Delaney decided she'd drop that subject for now and get back to more important matters.

"Where are the weapons?"

"He wouldn't say."

She snorted. "Well, that's damn inconvenient of him. What do you need me to do?"

"I told Rico that I had you wrapped around my little finger and that you'd do anything for me because you love me so much."

Delaney's eyes widened, but she didn't say anything. She didn't *love* Jack. That would be impossible. It was too soon. They barely knew each other. Yet, Delaney couldn't deny that she did have feelings for him. Those feelings seemed to grow and flourish each time they were together. But they were far too new to identify. She let herself consider the possibilities for a second, then dismissed the fanciful thoughts.

"I bet he was stupid enough to buy that," she said with a slight grin.

"Yeah, stupid," he said, his expression blank as an uncomfortable silence came over them.

She thought her joke would alleviate the tension, but instead it had backfired. Delaney didn't have time to ponder why. She had a case to solve. If they could descend upon the shipment as it was being loaded into the vans, then they'd catch David Rico in the act.

"How many vans are needed?"

"Five should do it," he said.

"Okay, I have a lot of phone calls to make. Hopefully McMillan can get what we need," she said.

Jack nodded. "You'll have to do it on the way to my house. Once inside, we won't be able to discuss the case beyond planning."

"Why?" she asked, tilting her head.

"Because we're already being watched."

"I don't see anyone."

"Trust me, they're there." He reached for her elbow and led her down the dock. "Time to play a couple in love," he said, swinging her around in his arms and planting a scorching kiss on her mouth.

When Jack finally released her, Delaney was breathless and her legs were doing their best wet-noodle impression. He reached out and gently caressed her cheek, something he seemed to love doing. Delaney felt the tremor in his fingertips all the way to her toes. Jack brushed her loose brown hair back off her face, curling it around her ear, while lingering on the fleshy part of her lobe.

His blue eyes heated as he watched her. Something had shifted. His expression seemed calm while his eyes remained turbulent. "Jack, is this the acting part?" she asked, needing to know.

He stiffened beside her, then grasped her elbow again as he led her to the car. "We have to get out of here before they become suspicious."

Delaney hid the disappointment she felt. What had she expected him to do, declare his love? She shook herself internally for being so stupid. This wasn't some fairy tale where love at first sight existed. Real lives were at stake. Luckily, Jack hadn't forgotten that, even if she had momentarily.

HOW COULD THE damn woman believe that he was acting after the night they spent together? Maybe to her the whole thing was a performance. The thought left a sour taste in Jack's mouth. Could he have been so wrong about Delaney?

His instincts might be rusty, but he didn't believe they'd completely failed him. She felt something for him, even if she didn't want to. And it was more than obvious that Delaney didn't *want* to care.

Well, too damn bad. She should've thought about that before they slept together.

Jack's lips still tingled from touching hers. He could taste the sweetness on his tongue that was uniquely Delaney's. He sure had it bad. How had he gotten himself into this mess? And better yet, how was he going to get himself out?

He had no doubt that once this assignment was over Delaney would do everything in her power to get away from him. Physically, she wanted him, but she continued to keep her emotional distance. She was scared to let him in and that fear would make her run. Jack couldn't let that happen. He wasn't sure how he was going to convince her to stay and give them a chance, but he'd figure something out.

THEY DROVE NORTH up Pacific Coast Highway to Malibu. Delaney called McMillan, so that he could make sure everything was in place. He'd e-mail her tomorrow in the late afternoon with the details prior to getting on the plane to Phoenix.

Jack's home overlooked the ocean from one of the many

hilltops. He had high-powered movie moguls and celebrities for neighbors, along with hippies who'd moved in during the sixties.

"I can't believe you're selling this place and moving to Phoenix. Won't you miss the ocean? The excitement? The glamour?"

He glanced at her, then back at the road as he wound his way through the neighborhood to reach his driveway. "I will miss the Pacific, but I can come out and see it anytime I want. It's not going anywhere. Besides, I like the idea of living in the quiet desert. As for the excitement and the glamour..." His mouth twisted wryly. "Glamour is an illusion, much like fame. I have no use for it. To be honest, I've had about all the excitement I can handle in one lifetime."

"I suppose Arizona is pretty cool, once you get used to the summers. Hell doesn't have anything on Phoenix in July and August." She grinned as they pulled in to the garage.

Jack leaned over and brushed her cheek with his lips. The line between pretend and reality blurred in her mind. What was real? Was anything truly happening between them or had it all been one big performance? Delaney could no longer keep up the pretense that Jack meant nothing to her.

"What would you like to do, since it's turned in to a waiting game?" she asked, stepping out of the vehicle before he could come around the car and open the door for her.

Jack grinned. "We can order some take-out or I can see what I can scrounge up in the kitchen. The view here isn't half-bad at sunset and we wouldn't have to fight for a table. Afterward, there are a few errands I need to take care of. Hopefully they won't take too long." His smile faded.

"I could use a shower," she said tightly, not missing the sudden change in his demeanor.

His eyes fastened on her bikini-clad body. "That can be arranged."

Delaney ignored the heat flaring between them as she walked toward the house. She didn't like the fact that Jack was keeping things from her. And why all of a sudden did he have errands to run? He hadn't mentioned anything earlier. It seemed odd that they'd popped up after their meeting with Rico.

They strolled to the door, pretending not to notice the vehicle parked down the lane. It hadn't taken Rico's goons long to set up surveillance. They'd probably done so before the meet. Delaney squashed the urge to call in the ATF and have them arrested. They were too close to making this a successful mission. She couldn't allow her emotions to get the better of her.

Jack opened the door and stepped back for her to enter. Floor-to-ceiling glass windows made up the far wall, giving the home's occupants an unhindered view of the Pacific below. An open floor plan led from the dining area into a modest kitchen and onto the living room beyond. Cream carpet covered the floors, accenting the pale walls.

While Jack's desert home was swathed with masculine shades, this one was light and airy, welcoming the ocean and all its natural beauty inside.

Delaney toed off her shoes, so she didn't track dirt through the house.

"You don't have to do that," Jack said, beside her ear. "I didn't buy this house to have my guests stand on ceremony. I want you to be comfortable. Besides, the new owners plan to replace all the carpeting, when they move in next month."

"I'd feel better with my shoes off."

"Suit yourself." He watched her for a few seconds before moving onto the kitchen. "In the past, I made use of this home quite a bit. My social life has died down as of late."

"Is that so?" she asked, incredulity filling her voice.

He turned, catching her gaze. "Yes, it is."

Something inside of her melted a fraction more.

"Can I get you anything to drink?"

"Wine would be nice, if you have it. If not, I'll take water." Delaney covered the short distance separating the kitchen from the wraparound living room.

Jack padded over the carpeted floor, his shoes suddenly MIA. Two wineglasses dangled from his fingertips as he watched her stare out at the ocean.

"I'm not sure I'd ever be able to sell this place," she said, meaning it as she reached for one of the glasses.

Jack moved beside her, staring at the lapping waves. "It's just a house, love. I can get another if I want."

Delaney glanced at his strong features, lingering on his firm mouth. "So why has your social life slowed?" she asked, feigning disinterest, but hoping he said it was because of her.

"You grow tired of the same experiences over time." He took a sip of wine and swallowed, running his tongue over his lips in appreciation. "What used to interest me no longer does. I'd rather let go of what's not working, than to cling in hopes that things will change."

"That makes sense. It's a very astute observation on your part."

"Thank you." He didn't hide the sarcasm in his voice. "You seem surprised I'm capable of such deep thoughts."

She canted her head. "I suppose I am, but probably not for the reasons you think." Delaney gave him what she hoped was a considering expression. "I've just never met a man who's ever given those types of things that much thought."

He grinned, his dimples matching pinpoints in his cheeks. "Sounds like you've been hanging around the wrong men."

"Isn't that the truth," Delaney muttered under her breath. She'd never met anyone like Jack Gordon. Prior to meeting him, she'd have sworn men like him didn't really exist outside of the movies. Unrealistic expectations, had she had them? Hanging here with Jack made her realize she'd always aimed low.

They stood, staring out the window, enjoying the companionable silence for several minutes.

"Can I ask you something, Jack?"

"Sure."

"Have you ever sold weapons to Somalia?"

He paused. "Why do you want to know?"

"Just curious," she offered. Why couldn't he just answer the question?

"I thought you wanted to take a shower," he said finally.

"I did. I mean I do."

Jack pointed down the hall. "There are two bedrooms that are en suite. You can use either bathroom. I'll make a call to Monty's and have them deliver a large pizza."

"Thanks," she said, then headed away.

"Delaney," he called out as she reached the bedroom door.

She stopped and looked back. He was still watching her. "Yes."

"I've never done any deals with that country."

Delaney gave him a quick smile. "Thank you."

"You're welcome," he replied, looking as if he wanted to say more.

Jack didn't know why Delaney had asked about Somalia, but he knew damn well that it had nothing to do with curiosity. The question had meant something to her—and so had his answer. Maybe someday she'd trust him enough to tell him why.

He listened as the shower came on in the master bath. His shaft hardened instantly as he imagined Delaney naked beneath the wet spray, droplets of water gliding over her skin, clinging to her lashes.

He stared longingly down the hall. What would she do if he joined her? Kick him out? Shoot him? Or would she let him join her, knowing there were two people down the hill recording their every move for Rico.

The urge to take, to claim, roared through him. Jack stepped back as he acknowledged he wanted to show the scumbag just who Delaney belonged to. What would Rico do once he saw her spread beneath him on the floor, his body riding hers into oblivion? Would he back off and leave her alone or would he desire her more? Jack wasn't sure, but he was willing to try anything in order to keep her safe.

Like making love to her would be such a hardship.

He picked up the phone and ordered dinner. Glancing at his watch he calculated he'd have just enough time to eat and enjoy the sunset before he had to go. There was no telling how long it would take him to reach Long Beach, California. Knowing the traffic on the 405 freeway, it could be two hours.

He wasn't looking forward to this meet with David Rico, but what choice did he have? He couldn't let the man get his hands on Delaney. As good an agent as she was, she was no match for Rico.

Jack didn't want to think about what he may have to do for the scumbag in order to keep Delaney safe, or how many years of his life it was going to cost him if he got caught. All he could hope for was that in the end, Delaney understood why he'd chosen to keep her out of the loop. Even if she never did, Jack knew he was doing the right thing.

The spray from the shower continued to flow in the background. More than once Jack found himself walking down the hall, only to turn back at the last minute.

Varying impulses battled for dominance. The urge to protect was nearly as strong as the urge to take. Jack stood in the middle of the hall, body shaking. What in the hell had she done to him? He'd never been like this. Indecision gripped him. He stormed back into the kitchen.

As much as he wanted to join Delaney in the shower, there wasn't time—at least not for what he wanted to do. It would have to wait until he returned. Unfortunately with Rico, there was a chance this would be a one-way trip.

12

DELANEY FOLLOWED Jack down the 405 freeway, heading south. She had no idea where he was going, but doubted errands would take him this far from home. She was grateful that he'd driven the rental car and left the keys to his car hanging on a hook near the door.

She'd had to wait a few minutes before she could leave. Concern had quickly turned to fear that she wouldn't be able to find him, but in the end, she'd somehow managed. Thank goodness for L.A. traffic.

It was challenging to keep an eye on his car, particularly while remaining three car lengths back and two over, but she'd done it. Delaney was positive Jack hadn't spotted her. He continued south until he reached the 710 freeway, then followed it to the Queen Mary. Why was he going there?

Delaney stared at the giant ship. Once a luxury liner used for crossing the Atlantic before commercial air travel, the ship now housed a hotel, restaurants and an art gallery.

She watched Jack pull in to the nearly full lot and park near a familiar black Escalade. The pizza in her stomach curdled, when she spotted Rico. Why was Jack meeting him without her? She didn't like the answer that popped in to her mind.

He got out of the vehicle at the same time David Rico exited. They moved to the back of the Escalade and began to talk. Delaney wished that she knew what they were saying, not that it mattered, since it was apparent that some other deal had been struck while they were on the boat.

She drove past the entrance, grateful for the cover of darkness, then circled back and pulled in far away from the two men. Several cars followed behind her, filling in the lot. She pocketed the keys then slipped out of the car, using the other parked vehicles around her for cover.

Delaney managed to get within two car lengths, then stopped, afraid Rico's goons or Jack might spot her. She strained to hear their conversation. When she realized she still couldn't, Delaney dropped to the ground and began to crawl forward on her stomach, inch by inch. Her hand landed in something wet and gooey. She cringed, but kept going.

"I knew you wouldn't pass up the money," Rico said.

"Hell, no, I'd be a fool to pass on that kind of cash," Jack said. "But just so you know, I wouldn't do it for a penny less than fifty thousand."

Delaney frowned.

"A man after my own heart." Rico snickered.

"When do I start?" Jack asked.

"Tonight was a test to see if you'd show up." Rico glanced around the lot, then looked back at Jack. "Tomorrow night I have a shipment coming in that I need relocated. It's smaller than the one we discussed today, but still substantial. If you manage to get the job done, I'll allow you to move up."

"I thought this was a one-time deal," Jack said.

"Why would you think that?"

Jack didn't answer.

Delaney's stomach rebelled. Jack was playing both sides? How could she be so wrong about him? She'd given her word to McMillan that they could trust him, but now...

Pain that shouldn't exist enveloped her. How could Jack do this to her? Anger trampled the hurt and pushed her into a standing position. She brushed the dirt and rocks from her hands and clothes.

She wouldn't let Jack and whatever side deal he'd worked out with Rico blow her case. She stepped forward out of the darkness, fear beating at her breast until both men could see her.

Rico noticed her first. "Ah, my dear. To what do we owe the pleasure?"

Jack stiffened, but otherwise didn't react.

"I was worried that my partner might try to cut me out of the deal. I see that my suspicions were well-founded," she said. Her gaze hardened as it slid over Jack. "It's my family who owns the vans, not Jack's. I'm taking the most risks. I like money just as much as he does and don't want to have to fly for the rest of my life."

"Ignore her," Jack insisted. "She's a woman who's never done business in this arena." He turned to Delaney and his eyes narrowed in warning. "I told you to wait at home for me."

"While you screw me out of my share. I don't think so," she hissed.

RICO STOOD BACK, watching the interaction between these two. This was better than he'd hoped. They obviously both loved each other, even though they tried to hide it. He laughed to himself. This was beyond perfect. Love made the most sane individuals behave foolishly. It was also volatile enough that he'd be able to use it to his advantage when the time came.

He turned to the woman. The anger and outrage she displayed was real. He'd use that to manipulate her into his bed. Might as well get the added enjoyment of her flesh, before he killed her.

"Well, now that we've established who's really in charge, you might as well join us," he said. She'd made it abundantly clear that he'd no longer need Jack Gordon. It would simply be a matter of finding the right time to dispose of him. "What's your name, pretty flight attendant?"

"Delaney," she answered.

"Delaney," Rico repeated. "Nice. It suits you." He reached out and touched her hair, then skimmed the side of her neck.

Jack's fists clenched, but he didn't move to stop him. Rico smiled to himself, enjoying this game more than most. He wondered how far he could go before Jack snapped, giving him all the reason he'd need to kill him now.

Jack took a step back and appeared to rein in his temper. Pity that. David was tempted to prod him again, but decided it was neither the time nor the place. There was work to do. He needed the main shipment moved out of Los Angeles. It was getting far too hot to stay. If the authorities found the merchandise before he could sell it at auction, he'd lose his chance to move up and, worse yet, David would have to answer to his investors. He shuddered at the thought.

"I was just telling Jack about a smaller job I want him to do for me, but it can wait until you deliver the vans. Jack tells me you're flying out tomorrow evening to pick them up in Phoenix."

"That's right," she said, ignoring Jack.

"Wonderful. I'll expect them to be outside the Marina shipyard the following day. Don't disappoint me." Rico nodded to his bodyguards. One stepped forward and opened the door to the Escalade. David entered without a backward glance. It was going to be so easy to convince those two that they couldn't trust each other. Their emotions made it child's play. In the end, maybe they'd kill each other and save him the trouble.

JACK WAS SO MAD he couldn't see straight. He'd come here to save her, and instead she'd played right in to Rico's hands.

"How did you get here?" he asked after Rico pulled away.

"I followed you. And it's a good thing I did or I wouldn't have found out you were playing both sides." Her face mottled.

"Playing both sides? Is that what you think was going on here?" His jaw clenched and he could feel it begin to tic. She thought he was betraying her, when all he'd wanted to do was save her sweet ass. Jack shoved his hands into his pockets as the pain from her distrust ripped at his gut.

"I heard you. I heard every word." Delaney's voice cracked. "So don't stand there and try to deny it."

Jack wasn't about to deny anything. He didn't have to explain himself or his actions to her or anyone else. So why did he feel the need to? "Where is my car or did you take a cab here?"

"I parked it at the far end."

"Give me the keys."

Delaney took a step back. "Wh-what about the rental?"

She could've gotten them both killed and the only thing she could think about was the damn rental car. Jack cursed under his breath. "Delaney, don't make me repeat myself."

She dipped into her pocket and withdrew the keys, tossing them to him, instead of handing them over. Delaney was staying out of arm's reach, which was probably good, until he got his temper in check—not that Jack would ever hurt her.

"I'll phone the rental agency and tell them where they can pick up the car," he said, walking in the direction she'd indicated.

He needed to put some distance between them. The fear he'd felt when he saw her pop up on the other side of the car had left an acute ache behind. For a second his mind had refused to believe what his eyes were telling him. Jack had wanted nothing more than to whisk her away and lock her somewhere safe until this job ended. The fear had affected him far more deeply than he cared to admit.

DELANEY STOOD unable to move. Her emotions were in turmoil. On one hand, she knew what she'd heard. On the other, there was Jack's misdirected anger. He had no right being angry with her. She hadn't lied and gone behind his back to meet in secret with Rico. He'd done that and she wouldn't allow him to turn this situation around and pin the blame on her.

This was her case, darn it. He had no right trying to work out a separate deal just because Rico offered him a lot of money. Jack had enough money already. Why did he need more at her expense?

"Are you coming?" he shouted, without looking at her.

Delaney straightened, then glanced around the dark parking lot. It wasn't going to do her any good to stay here. She'd have to report these latest events to McMillan, who would probably never trust her word again.

She slipped out her cell phone and pressed a button. Special-Agent-in-Charge Anderson answered. "Uh, is Group Supervisor McMillan there?" she asked, her voice whisper quiet.

"I've taken charge of this mission. What do you need, Agent Carter?"

Delaney debated whether to tell Anderson about the meeting between Rico and Jack. She knew it was the correct thing to do, but it still didn't feel right. "McMillan said you had a man ready to protect Jack Gordon," she said instead.

"Yes."

"We need them. Rico has made contact. I believe Jack's life may be in danger."

There was a pause on the other end of the line. "*May* be in danger, but you're not sure?"

"That is correct, sir." She tried and failed to keep the exasperation out of her voice.

"Jack's a big boy. I'm sure he'll be fine," Anderson said.

"Sir, I wish you'd reconsider. Gordon has done everything he promised the Bureau that he'd do. It's only fair that we do the same for him."

"Do I need to repeat myself, Agent Carter?"

"No, sir."

"I suggest rather than worrying about Jack Gordon that you worry about how you're going to explain that videotape, when you put in for your promotion next month."

Cold swept through Delaney. This was the second time in so many minutes that she felt the acid bite of betrayal. The last place she expected it to come from was the Bureau. "One more thing, sir. Did you ever intend to protect Jack Gordon?" she asked, before she could stop herself.

"You are a quick learner." Anderson laughed. "Phone when you *really* need backup," he said, then disconnected the call.

THE RIDE HAD BEEN TENSE and beyond uncomfortable. Jack was grateful that Delaney had held her silence. He was afraid he'd stop and shake her for putting herself in such danger.

Hell, it was a miracle that Rico hadn't cut his losses and walked away. He must really need those vans, Jack thought, admitting that they were the only reason that he and Delaney were still breathing.

He pulled in to the driveway and shut off the engine. Delaney jumped out before he'd even managed to remove the key from the ignition. He stepped out of the car and hit the alarm before walking to the house and opening the door. He stepped aside to allow Delaney entry, half expecting her to slam the door in his face.

She didn't. In fact, she didn't look at him at all. Instead, she remained deceptively calm as she crossed the threshold. Jack followed behind her and locked the door.

Delaney spun on him, the second he'd finished. "How dare you stab me in the back with Rico."

"Me, stab you? If you ever do anything that stupid again, I'll take you over my knee," he said, stepping closer.

Delaney's eyes widened at the threat, but otherwise didn't back down. "Don't you try to change the subject. I recognize a double-cross when I see one."

Jack stalked toward her. He didn't stop coming until his hands rested beside her head and caged her with his body. "Double-cross? It's nice to know you think so little of me." His lips thinned.

Delaney recoiled, but didn't recant her words.

Jack leaned in until he could feel the heat of her anger radiating off her body. Her gaze dropped to his lips and the rage shifted to a wave of desire. His groin tightened. Why did he respond so brutally to a woman who refused to trust him? He slammed his palm against the wall in frustration.

"For your information," he said, his voice becoming raspy under the effort to talk, "I went there to save you."

"Save me?" She shook her head.

"Yes, save you. It was either work for him or hand you over."

"What? I don't understand."

"Then let me spell it out for you. Rico wants you. Bad. Bad enough to kill, but he can't have you."

"Why?" she asked.

"Because I want you more," he barked, a second before his lips crushed down upon hers.

DELANEY'S HANDS moved to Jack's chest to push him away. The second she encountered his heated flesh, her fingers curled, clutching the front of his shirt, while their tongues battled for supremacy. Warmth exploded in her stomach as Jack deepened the embrace, turning savage in his pursuit.

Anger and something far more powerful enveloped her. She wanted to hurt him, while at the same time pull him near. His mouth was making her crazy. She couldn't think, couldn't breathe, only feel.

Delaney groaned, pressing her body forward until her sensitive breasts scraped the hard, flat slab of his chest. His musky scent enveloped her. Her nails dug into his shoulders as she struggled to get closer.

Jack's hands moved from the wall and Delaney heard a rip as he tore her shirt off her body, then moved to undo her pants. He fingers returned seconds later to tease her nipples through the lace of her bra. Jack pulled the straps from her shoulders and deftly unhooked the clasp, trapping her arms. His mouth replaced his fingers and Delaney was lost.

"Mine," he growled, nipping her flesh in a sting of pleasure-pain.

Her head fell back against the wall as Jack sucked and laved her breasts. Gone was the gentle lover she'd met back in Phoenix. He'd been replaced by a man possessed, who was bent on possessing her, too. Jack released the hardened pebble, then yanked her pants down. He pulled, taking her shoes and underwear with them, deftly tossing the items behind him.

His mouth came back to hers, searching, hungry, then Delaney felt her feet leave the ground. Jack braced her back against wall, only long enough to free his cock and sheathe himself with a condom. Then he was inside her, moving like a piston.

She knew instinctively that he was using his body to punish her in a way he never would. Delaney whimpered in need as each thrust pushed her up the wall, driving her passions further over the edge.

"I cannot believe that you followed me," he groaned in her

ear, then rolled his hips for emphasis, spearing her deep. "You could've gotten us killed. You could've gotten *you* killed."

Delaney found it difficult to focus with the pressure from her impending orgasm building inside of her. Jack's body shuddered beneath her fingertips. She could feel his heart pounding in his chest. Sweat dripped down the side of his face, leaving his hair slick. The aroma of sex filled the air.

"Are you listening to me?" he asked, then nipped her earlobe to focus her attention.

"Yes, I'm listening," she told him. Her head was spinning from the kiss and his intensity.

"Don't you understand that I don't want anything to happen to you?" He ground his body into hers, brushing her clit in the process.

Delaney cried out.

"I couldn't bear it, if anything happened to you," he declared, his voice breaking with unspoken emotion.

Something inside Delaney melted at his words and tears prickled her eyes. A second later, her orgasm roared through her. She shouted Jack's name, tensing in his arms, her body exploding into a million tiny nerve endings. Jack gripped her bottom and thrust in a frenzied movement, then bellowed, following her to completion.

His lungs labored as he slowly lowered Delaney to her feet. "I'm sorry if I hurt you," he said quietly, brushing his nose tenderly to hers.

"You didn't." Her body trembled as the aftershocks of pleasure coursed through her.

"I need you to promise me something," he said, his voice serious and his gaze unwavering.

Delaney brushed her hair away from her face. "What is it?"

The equivalent of Jack's heart was in his eyes when he answered. "To never scare me like that ever again."

13

"Are you ready?" Jack asked, squeezing her hand in reassurance as they stood in a deserted gate area in Los Angeles International Airport. White lines bracketed his sensual mouth, the only indication that despite his placid expression he was feeling the pressure of the impending deal.

"I'm fine," Delaney lied smoothly. So many things could go wrong once they retrieved the vans from Phoenix and brought them back here to L.A. That was only one of the reasons she was concerned. The other had to do with Jack. He'd explained the deal Rico had offered him after they'd made love last night.

Delaney was still reeling that Jack had cared enough to risk his life and his freedom to protect her. They'd been through so much together in such a short period of time, but that still didn't stop her from worrying that once this case was finished, she and Jack would go their separate ways.

"We have a few minutes before we have to get to the gate. Rico's men will be waiting for us outside the Marina shipyard tomorrow when we get back. Your people will probably catch Rico watching nearby. He doesn't trust anyone enough to let them take care of the loading alone, so you're worrying for nothing."

"You're probably right. I'm sure the deal will go down smoothly." Delaney rolled her stiff shoulders.

"Why don't we take a short walk?" Jack suggested in an obvious attempt to ease her tension.

"Do you think we have time?" she asked, glancing at her watch.

"Sure, if we make it quick." Jack winked.

They strolled down the winding hallway that led to gate eleven. The last of the flights for that area had come in four hours ago and nothing was scheduled to leave until tomorrow. Two doors opened onto deserted jetways. Delaney strode to the nearest one and punched in a code after swiping her ID.

The door opened and Jack stepped aside for her to enter. Always the gentleman, she thought wryly, secretly loving every minute of it. The jetway was dark and musty, as if it had sat unused in the sea air for too long. Delaney shivered from the dampness, but didn't turn on the light. Jack slipped his arm around her, enveloping her in his body heat.

For a moment, Delaney allowed herself to sink in to his strength and draw comfort from his presence. After tomorrow, she probably wouldn't see Jack again. Sadness cloaked her.

Over the past few days she'd come to look forward to spending time with him. She didn't want to go back to sitting home alone on the weekends, watching television and eating ice cream out of the carton.

In a few short days, Jack had shown her possibilities. He'd introduced her to a life outside of work and Delaney wasn't ready to give that up and return to the status quo. She'd realized that last night. Although the thought scared her, the fear wasn't enough to change her mind.

She took a step and felt her SIG Sauer 229 brush her leg as they strolled. The pistol's weight was light enough that it didn't hinder her ability to walk…too much. She'd checked the clip earlier to make sure it held frangibles.

Although not without risks, it was the safest ammo to fire

on a plane and would disintegrate when it hit the target, while leaving a shallow widespread wound behind. The last thing they needed was a decompression at thirty thousand feet. She shuddered at the thought. Luckily, there should be no reason to draw her weapon. She adjusted the ankle holster.

"What do you have there?" Jack asked from behind her.

"An insurance package for when we get to Phoenix," she said, repositioning the pistol. It wasn't exactly comfortable, but it was a lot better than being unarmed. Which to Delaney's mind, wasn't an option.

The agents pretending to be rental van employees would already be in place. It wasn't much of a backup, considering the manpower Rico had, but it would have to do.

"Are we set?" Jack asked, as they reached the end of the jetway. He brushed his chin on top of her head, while pulling her against his body. Again, his warmth comforted her, along with his distinct masculine scent. Delaney didn't think that she'd ever get that fragrance out of her mind. The man smelled incredible.

"Yes, I think so," she said, turning in his arms, so she could loop her fingers around his neck.

Jack's lips met hers in a tender kiss. There was no fire, only a simmering connection of familiarity that held unspoken promises. He pulled back slightly, until he could look in to her eyes. The airport lights bathed the jetway in ghostly light, leaving everything shadowed, intimate.

"It'll be okay, Delaney," he said reassuringly. "I promise." He brushed her lower lip with the pad of his thumb and kissed her again.

Delaney took a shaky breath and nodded, allowing his touch to propel her worries away. Oh, how she longed to be back in Jack's bed, their naked bodies clinging as they burned up the sheets.

"I'll make sure Rico doesn't get anywhere near you." His arms tightened fractionally as if he didn't want to let her go. "Once this is finished we can start over like we talked about."

Delaney's eyes widened. Did Jack still mean it? Could they start over? It seemed like a lifetime ago since they'd discussed the idea in his kitchen. Would they even live long enough to try? All good questions that she couldn't afford to think about right now. They'd distract her when she needed to be at her best.

"Let's concentrate on getting through this ordeal," she said, reluctantly putting some distance between them.

Jack frowned slightly. "I only wanted to say—"

"Later." Delaney cut him off by pressing her finger to his lips. She knew it was cowardly, but she wasn't prepared to hear what he had to say. Not yet. Perhaps not ever. She didn't think her heart could take it. His tongue flicked out, scorching her and hardening her nipples. Delaney jerked her hand back. "You don't play fair."

Jack didn't say a word as an unholy light filled his eyes. There was knowledge glowing in those blue depths, along with awareness and…possession.

Panic struck Delaney as she realized she liked the way he was looking at her. It made her skin heat while at the same time culled the hope that she kept hidden away. The power Jack had over her was frightening and enthralling in equal measure.

"We'd better get back or we'll miss the plane," she reminded him, sliding her hands down his arms, tracing the long lines of his muscles under his shirt with her fingertips, memorizing every contour in case this was her last opportunity to touch him. Despite hoping otherwise, Delaney knew there was a very good possibility that was the truth.

Everyone knew fairy tales were for suckers and fools. Delaney was neither. So why did she want so badly to believe?

She and Jack walked down the main corridor of Terminal One. It was early evening and the airport was packed with travelers busily making their way to various destinations. The tinkling of cell phones rang out in the crowd, playing a digital version of Marco Polo as they weaved their way through the people.

Travelers bumped her, sending her teetering back. Jack reached out and clutched her hand to steady her. They arrived at Gate Seven a few moments later. A crowd gathered around Gate Nine as the people deplaned temporarily blocking her view. When the crowd parted, Delaney's gaze moved back to Gate Seven. Her eyes widened as she saw passengers boarding the aircraft.

Crap! She was late.

Jeremy came walking up the jetway, peering through the crowd. He waved when he spotted her.

People trickled down the jetway and milled by the gate agent behind the podium.

"Where have you been?" Jeremy stood at the top of the jetway frowning. "We're getting ready to push. I couldn't cover for you any longer. The pilots are already in the cockpit. Hurry and get aboard, I have a hot date lined up in Phoenix." He tapped his watch.

Delaney forced herself to smile. "Shall we?" she said.

They boarded the plane. The bright overhead lights gave everyone a sickly pallor. Delaney watched from the forward entry as Jack took his seat in first class.

She turned to greet the next passengers boarding. "Good evening, welcome aboa—" The words faded as she caught sight of David Rico and his bodyguard Tony strolling down the jetway toward the plane.

Rico grinned like a mongoose eyeing a cobra when their eyes met. Delaney forced herself to remain in place, when every fiber called for her retreat. What was he doing here? He was supposed to meet them tomorrow night.

His gaze glided over her, pausing at her breasts. Delaney hid her disgust. Rico ran a hand through his perfectly cut hair. It sprang back in place like a coil. "Fancy running in to you here. What are the odds?"

Slim, Delaney thought. "I don't understand," she said, looking over her shoulder toward Jack, who hadn't noticed Rico yet. "What are you doing here? We're on our way to pick up the vans now."

He smirked. "I was never very good at waiting."

"Are you coming with us to get them?" Delaney asked, needing to know exactly why he was here. Did he not trust them to follow through? Had their cover been blown?

David glanced at Tony, then he shrugged. "There's been a slight change of plans."

This wasn't good. A change of plans at the last minute was never good. How would she notify McMillan, or Anderson for that matter?

There'd be no way he could get more ATF agents on the ground at Sky Harbor Airport in Phoenix without a heads-up. The best she could hope for was that McMillan had assigned someone to watch them and that they'd spotted Rico and Tony boarding the plane. Delaney doubted she could be that lucky.

Why hadn't she considered that Rico might change the plans under possible worst-case scenarios? They'd been so sure he would wait for them that they'd gotten sloppy. And now their negligence may cost people their lives.

Delaney paused as a horrifying thought crossed her mind. If he was here, then where was the merchandise? According to Jack, Rico kept his shipments close. At least close enough that he could reach them within a few minutes if need be.

Her gaze drifted out the window to the crew loading the

plane. She couldn't see what was happening on the ground, beyond a lot of movement. He couldn't be that stupid. She stared at Rico and considered breaking cover. There were too many unknown variables on a flight.

What if there happened to be a sky marshal onboard or an off-duty cop? So many things could go wrong in the air, and if they did, it wasn't like backup could race in to help. Thirty thousand feet was a long way to drop without a net.

Delaney took a deep breath. No sense in getting ahead of herself. Rico had given her no indication that the weapons were here. The last thing she needed was to raise the alarm only to find out that she'd been wrong.

She took a step back and felt the SIG Sauer pistol brush her ankle. It may not be much, but it was all she had. In the end, Delaney knew she couldn't scrap the mission. There was more at stake than a plane load of people. There was the safety of thousands to consider.

Delaney pushed the thought out of her mind and concentrated on the facts. All she had to do was keep everyone calm for an hour and fifteen minutes. Perhaps if she kept Rico's attention focused on her, then even the two flight attendants would remain blissfully unaware of how much danger they were in. After that, they'd be in Phoenix and she'd be able to contact the ATF.

Maybe she could slip a note to the pilots? She peered into the cockpit.

Rico leaned past her. "Hey, Tom, long time no see. How's the new boat?"

The first officer turned and grinned. "I'm loving it, thanks. Great seeing you again, Dave. We'll try to give you a smooth ride."

"You do that," Rico said, facing Delaney once more.

Delaney's stomach clenched. So much for slipping the

pilots a note. Rico had managed to get a man in place in the cockpit. This was getting better and better.

"Are we meeting the package?" she asked, hoping her assumption was wrong.

Rico looked out the window and waved to the rampers loading the plane. "No, I see my luggage being loaded right now."

"On the plane?" Delaney strangled on the question. He truly was stupid or insane. Either way everyone's life was now in danger.

"That's normally where you put luggage too large to fit in the overhead bin."

"I don't think that's a good idea."

"Luckily, I'm not paying you to think. Just do your job and it'll be over before you know it. Remember, you have your passengers to consider." The threat was thinly veiled.

Delaney peered at the people who counted on her to keep them safe. There was no backing out. "You'd better take your seats, gentlemen," she said, noticing a few passengers' curious glances. "We'll be departing shortly." Delaney looked at Jack, who was now staring at Rico. He appeared to be about as happy as she felt.

Rico's bodyguard, Tony, sat toward the back, snagging an aisle seat. His eyes followed Barbie's ass like a bull after a matador's cape as she moved forward shutting overhead bins.

Delaney didn't like the way he watched her, but couldn't do anything about it at present. Rico remained in first class near Jack, but up and over one row. He, too, had taken an aisle seat.

To the casual observer, their seat selections appeared random, but Delaney knew they'd arranged themselves strategically. The flight was only half full with most of the passengers sitting up front and in the middle, but that still left fifty potential casualties.

"Flight attendants prepare for departure," the captain said.

The plane pushed back from the jetway. After a brief delay on the taxiway, the tower cleared them for departure. The plane's engines revved a second before the pilots released the brakes.

The beast lurched, then steadily increased speed. Delaney tried not to think about the cargo or how volatile it was as she sat in her brace position, clutching the seat belt. The aircraft banked right and then continued to climb, causing her ears to pop like champagne corks. As long as nothing else exploded, they'd be fine.

She took out her cart as soon as the plane leveled off and began her beverage service. The cart wobbled, refusing to cooperate as Delaney forced the heavy metal monstrosity down the aisle.

Twice the trolley almost rolled away from her, threatening to escape. She was convinced it would take a priest and an exorcism to fix it. *Not tonight, please.* Delaney muttered and kicked the wheel, stubbing her toe. She sucked in a pain-filled breath and hobbled on.

Somehow she'd managed to get her beverage service completed and returned to replenish the cart. Afterward, Delaney rounded the galley wall with a garbage bag in her hands prepared to pick up trash and nearly ran in to David Rico. He smiled and took a step forward. She stepped back.

Her gaze sought Jack, who was scowling in his seat. He kept glancing at his watch as if that would somehow make the plane fly faster.

"What do you want?" she asked Rico.

"To spend some time getting to know you."

She stiffened. "I have to get back to work." Delaney moved to go around him, but he blocked her escape.

"You can take a few minutes to talk to your business partner."

Delaney lost her temper, angry that he'd tried and succeeded in scaring her. "I can't believe you brought weapons on board. Are you insane?" she spluttered under her breath.

Rico backhanded her so fast that Delaney didn't have time to duck. Hell, it had happened so fast that no one seemed to notice. That is, no one but Jack, who hadn't taken his eyes off them. Delaney shook her head to clear it, and then stuttered to her feet in time to see Jack rise out of his seat.

She jerked her head in warning, sending pain screaming through her skull. Delaney didn't want to draw the attention of the passengers, and if Jack came up here there'd be a brawl. The metallic tang of blood filled her mouth where Rico had split the inside of her lip. She glared, willing Jack to stay put.

Jack paused, his body twitching in impotent fury, then he sat once more. His hands clenched the top of the seat back until his knuckles turned white. His normally handsome features had hardened, sending a shiver of fear down her spine.

Delaney had never seen that expression on Jack's face, not even when she'd told him the truth about her mission. He glared at David with hatred in his eyes. Her gaze left him to return to Rico. She leveled her attention on him and wiped away the blood with her fingertips, flicking it casually onto the galley floor.

Delaney lowered her voice so only he could hear her. "Anyone ever tell you that you hit like a girl?" she asked, goading him even when her mind railed against the act. She needed to keep him off balance, angry, but not homicidal.

David Rico raised his hand to hit her again, but stopped when he noticed passengers glancing their way. "You're lucky we have an audience," he said, lowering his hand to stroke her jaw.

No, you're the lucky one, Delaney thought.

"You have a smart mouth on you," he said, touching her lip where it had split, sending pain shooting down her neck.

She bit the inside of her cheek to keep from crying out.

"We'll finish this later when we have a little more—" he

looked around "—privacy. I can think of much better ways to keep that mouth of yours busy." His hand dropped lower, caressing her collarbone before releasing her.

Delaney's mind screamed, demanding that she recoil. She didn't. She refused to allow David Rico the satisfaction of seeing how much his touch repulsed her. If he thought she actually enjoyed his unwanted attention it may work to her benefit.

She looked past him down the aisle. Tony stood with his back to them, all his attention focused on Barbie. As if sensing that he was being watched, he turned and grinned, waggling his eyebrows like an idiot.

That didn't bode well for Barbie or anyone else's safety as long as these two were on this flight. Would Rico and Tony actually kill a planeload of innocent people over a weapons smuggling operation?

Even as Delaney asked herself the question, she already knew the answer. Yes, they would and not lose a night's sleep over it.

14

JACK SAT IN an aisle seat, rage swirling inside of him. His heart threatened to burst from his chest and he'd clenched his jaw so tight he'd actually heard a couple of teeth crack.

When Rico hit Delaney, Jack had come close to leaving his seat, so he could kill the man, even though it would've meant dying himself, since he had no doubt Rico was armed. For a split second, Jack hadn't cared. How dare he touch her? He'd promised Delaney that he would protect her. The bastard would pay. The only thing that had kept him in his seat was the plea Jack saw in Delaney's eyes. He couldn't help her if he was dead.

Delaney must have said something strong to provoke the bastard into using violence. Knowing his woman, it could have been anything. Jack stilled as he considered what he'd just thought. *His woman.* He'd never considered anyone as *his* before. He mulled over that realization for a moment. Somehow with Delaney it just seemed right.

She was the first person who'd ever truly "needed" him, even if she didn't fully see it yet. Delaney was stubborn to the point of mule-headed. Her mouth could wither a rose. She would fight him with her last breath before admitting that she cared or that she was wrong.

She was frustrating and delectable, infuriating and insatiable, a combustible combination that left him panting for more. Yet, even with all that, she brought a smile to his face and actually made him want to be a better man. All Jack knew for sure was that he wasn't ready to let all that go. Not yet.

Maybe not ever.

He turned to locate Tony. The goon seemed glued into place and overly preoccupied with the blond looker in the back. That may be a good thing when Jack made his move.

He needed to wait until David Rico was closer. He didn't want to take the chance of anyone being hurt, especially Delaney. Jack couldn't lose her, not after all they'd been through.

His gaze returned to her. He could see that her lip had begun to swell. Blood still seeped from the wound, but Delaney ignored it, keeping her eyes on Rico instead. Her gaze was steady and her stance loose, but Jack could see that was for show. Delaney was ready to pounce when the opportunity presented itself. Pride swelled within him.

Good girl, he thought. *Keep the bastard's attention so that I can sneak up on him and bash his head in.* His hands fisted and knuckles popped. Jack wanted Rico to suffer and bleed.

He looked out the window at the dark ground below to see if he could determine their location. Jack searched for city lights. A bright glow burned in the distance. He'd bet his savings that it was Tucson, not Phoenix. Not that it mattered, they just needed a runway to land the plane.

Why had Rico changed their plans after seeking their help in the first place? Did he suspect a setup? He must have or else he would've filled them in. He'd watched in horror as the men on the ground loaded the volatile cargo. They were riding on enough explosives to blow this plane into orbit.

Fear settled into his gut, clutching it hard. He'd done several deals in his time with a lot of crazy people, but none as unpredictable as the one standing in the galley.

Rico was known for being unstable, but loading a plane

with explosives was out-and-out insane. Maybe that accounted for his sudden deviation from the plan. Jack prayed the change wasn't because Rico sensed deception. If that was the case, he and Delaney were both the walking dead.

He searched the faces around him as he attempted to come up with a plan. They needed something that would keep Rico busy, but not spook him into injuring passengers.

He had no doubt that the ATF had the Phoenix control tower following their progress, since the feds knew they were due in on this flight. The question was would they realize that Rico and Tony had boarded the aircraft in L.A., too?

"Rico," Jack called out, not exactly sure what he'd say once the man walked over to where he sat. They'd deviated so far from the arrangement that he needed to get some idea of what was happening before he could proceed.

David Rico turned away from Delaney and strolled down the aisle toward him. "What?"

Jack's nostrils flared as he reined in his temper. "I want to know what's happening. I think I deserve that much consideration."

Rico snorted. "You don't deserve a thing. The only reason I allowed you to come along was because I needed little Miss Sunshine's help procuring the vans." He hooked a thumb in Delaney's direction. "I didn't think she'd cooperate without you."

So he was going to cut him out of the deal. "Speaking of plans, why the change?" Jack asked, casually.

"I received word that the feds had all the roads out of town covered. You would've been able to get the vans in, but not back out. I found that unacceptable. By the way, you wouldn't know how they found out there was a shipment leaving, would you?" His gaze narrowed.

Jack remained impassive. "I don't like the direction this

conversation is headed. If the feds are on your ass, then you'd better take a closer look at the people around you."

"Oh, I am. You'd better hope I don't find out that you're the one behind the leak."

"My people are reliable." He glanced at Delaney for emphasis.

Rico followed his line of sight. "We'll see. Once we get on the ground, my people will unload the merchandise."

"What about us?" Jack asked, without inflection.

"The girl will come with me. We have unfinished business." Rico grinned. "You get to stay and explain to the feds, who will receive an *anonymous* tip about how you helped transport contraband."

Jack leveled his gaze on Rico. "What makes you think I'm going to sit here and allow you to hang me out to dry?"

Rico leaned in until their faces were mere inches apart. "Because if you don't, I'll kill her."

Fear pummeled him. Jack opened his mouth to speak.

"Don't bother," Rico warned, cutting him off. "I've seen the way you look at her. There's more than sex happening between you two. I knew it the day you gave me the boat."

The bastard thought he had the whole thing figured out. He'd be in for one hell of a wake-up call when he discovered Delaney was an agent for the ATF. Of course, when Rico did, she'd be dead. Hell, if she went with him at all, she was as good as dead. Jack's gut twisted. He couldn't allow that to happen. There had to be a way to stop the bastard before they reached Phoenix and he planned to find it.

DELANEY PULLED HER cart back out into the aisle. It worried her that she didn't know what Jack and Rico had discussed. She prayed Jack had remained cool. She started down the aisle, handing out free drinks to distract the passengers.

Jeremy spotted her and got up from a seat to retrieve his cart. Tony looked at him, then at Rico, who scowled and approached her.

"What do you think you're doing?" Rico asked. "We're going to land soon."

"I'm making sure the passengers are comfortable. That's my job."

He ran a hand through his hair and looked around. People watched their exchange. He turned back to her, anger simmering just below the surface. "Fine, but do it fast."

Delaney nodded at Jeremy to continue.

Suddenly, Rico smiled. The act made Delaney's skin crawl.

"What?" she asked.

He flicked his gaze over her. "I was thinking about how much I look forward to teaching you some manners after we land."

She frowned. "What do you mean?"

Rico laughed. "Go ask your boyfriend." He started to leave, but paused. "Oh, and while you're at it, you may want to say goodbye." With that he strolled down the aisle toward Tony.

Delaney's chest constricted. Goodbye? What was Rico talking about? She shoved the cart temporarily in front of the forward entry door and walked to where Jack waited. Their eyes met, blue clashing with brown. Delaney saw fear, concern and an abundance of rage swirling in his depths. She also saw…love. Something inside her soared, before reality stomped it with its dirty feet. There'd be time later to explore those emotions…she hoped.

"Want to tell me what you and Rico talked about?" she asked, her stomach tying itself into a pretzel.

"Not really."

"Jack?"

"He updated me on his schedule."

Delaney's interest perked. If they knew what he had in store, then it would be easier to stop him. "That's good news, right?"

Jack grunted. "You'd think, but it's not."

She took a deep breath and absorbed the chiseled masculine beauty of his face, committing it to memory...just in case. "Tell me. I need to know everything."

Rico and Tony were still too far away to overhear their conversation. Not that they seemed concerned one way or the other. The two men hadn't bothered to keep them apart. They mustn't care whether Jack told Delaney their idea. There could be only one reason for their cavalier attitude. Her blood chilled.

She considered the possibilities and didn't like what she came up with. "I take it he has people on the ground prepared to unload the cargo."

Jack nodded. "Yes, and I'm expendable. I have been since you announced that your *family* owned a van rental agency and you were taking the most risks. I can't say that I'm surprised."

"Expendable..." Delaney's gut clenched as she recalled the same word bantered about in McMillan's office. She looked at Jack and her heart actually ached with the thought of losing him.

"After he gets rid of me, I'm afraid you won't be far behind." Jack reached for her, his palm enveloping her hand. His thumb brushed her knuckles, soothing her nerves as no other balm could. "Listen, I won't let him take you. I plan to jump him before we land. If anything happens to me, fight like hell to get away from this bastard."

"Jack, don't talk like that. Nothing is going to happen to you as long as you don't do anything stupid."

He squeezed her hand until it bordered on pain. "Promise me, Delaney. Promise me that you won't let him touch you."

She gulped, tears springing suddenly to her eyes. "I promise." And she wouldn't let anything happen to Jack, either.

"Good." Jack gave her hand one final squeeze, then released her. "Now listen up. Here's what I know. When we get to Phoenix, Rico is going to have his men unload the cargo. He plans to take you and the munitions with him when he leaves."

"You said he considered you expendable. What does he plan to do to you?"

Jack laughed, the sound pain-filled. "I'm going to be here when the feds arrive. He thinks I'll be booked for aiding and abetting."

Delaney's gaze moved to Rico, who actually had the gall to wave at her. "So he plans to feed you to the lions."

"I'd say that about covers it. My guess is he'll shoot me first."

She glared at the gunrunner, imagining various scenarios that would allow her to unman him. "What does he intend to do with me after he gets the vans?"

Delaney looked at Jack and froze. The pain that was there in his face only moments ago had been replaced by rage. "I won't let him have you."

"Please, let me handle it. I mean it, Jack. We have people in place once we get to Phoenix. They were there to follow us and make sure the van pickup went smoothly. They may not be expecting Rico, but they won't let him get away. I'm trying to formulate a way to contact them ahead of time."

"Have you come up with anything yet?" Jack asked, knowing full well that she hadn't.

"No, but I will. I always do."

"Remember what I said, Delaney. I won't let him take you. Not as long as I have breath left in my lungs."

She sighed. "He won't. Just don't go getting yourself hurt or killed."

"You know me," he said, his lip curling in what she was sure was supposed to be a smile, but didn't quite make it.

Delaney stood, their eyes met one last time. "Jack, one more thing."

"Yes."

"Do you think Rico was lying about loading the arsenal onto the plane?" Not that it mattered, because it wouldn't change their current situation, but Delaney wanted to know their chances of making it onto the ground alive.

Jack washed a hand over his face. "I don't know. I saw them load something, but Rico is a damn good liar. One of the best I've ever encountered. He's also one of the most ruthless, but he doesn't strike me as suicidal."

"So I take it that's a yes."

He nodded. "Watch your back."

"You, too."

Rico came strolling up the aisle. "I trust you both have had time to say your goodbyes."

Delaney smirked. "Now why would we do that?"

His gaze hardened as he looked at Jack. "You did tell her what I told you. Right?"

"Verbatim."

"So why is she so chipper?"

Delaney chortled. "Haven't you ever heard that all flight attendants are hired for their sunny dispositions?"

"No." Rico jerked his head around. "And even if I had, I don't think you'd fall in to that category."

"Ouch! That hurts me here." She pressed a hand to her chest. "Just goes to show what you know." Delaney walked back to the galley to retrieve her cart for a final drink service. She shoved her hands into her pockets so Rico couldn't see them tremble.

She had made it two rows into her service when Delaney saw Tony head to the back galley where Barbie worked. Delaney couldn't seem to catch her breath as she watched Tony pull the curtain aside, exposing the back galley to everyone's line of sight.

Her heart thudded in her chest as he loomed over the flight attendant. Delaney couldn't hear what they were saying. Suddenly, Barbie grinned a "ya'll come on in" kind of greeting. She glanced at Delaney and winked before pulling the curtain closed.

She'd lost it. There was no other explanation for Barbie's bizarre behavior.

Delaney had to do something. She couldn't allow Tony to possibly hurt one of her crew members. Jeremy was still serving drinks, blissfully unaware of the unfolding situation. She set the brake on her trolley and squeezed past it, determined to stop Tony by any means necessary.

Rico stepped out from a seat, stopping her short.

"Get out of my way," Delaney warned, not bothering to consider the consequences.

"You need to return to work. Now."

She pointed to the back galley, her ears straining to hear over the engines' loud hum. "What does he think he's doing?"

"It's not your concern."

Delaney balled her fists.

"I said get back to your job."

"What if I refuse," she fired back.

"Fine." Rico pulled out a 9 mm Glock. "The next person I shoot will be on your conscience," he said, turning to choose a victim.

Passengers around them cried out.

Delaney's mind blanked as she focused on the barrel. How had he gotten that past security? Probably the same way he'd been able to load weapons onto a commercial flight—inside help.

"Wait!" Delaney grabbed his elbow. "Don't," she pleaded, hating the show of weakness. "It's okay, folks. He's a sky marshal," she said attempting to halt the panic.

"He doesn't look like a sky marshal to me," someone shouted. Rico glowered.

"He's not supposed to. He needs to blend in," Delaney lied.

Rico looked around the cabin, meeting the eyes of several people. "I'm here on official business, so get back to doing what you were doing," he shouted, then holstered his gun.

"Listen to the marshal, folks. There's nothing to see here," she assured.

"Are you going to go back to serving drinks like a good little girl?"

"Yes," she spit out between clenched teeth. Tears of frustration filled her eyes as she thought about Barbie in the back galley. She couldn't save her anymore than she could save these passengers, if Rico decided to kill them.

Delaney glanced at Jack as she passed and saw only compassion. She returned to her cart, kicking the lock to release the wheels so she could roll it down the aisle.

With quivering fingers she poured her drinks, her eyes glued to the back of the plane. Delaney saw Jeremy's head snap around to stare at the closed curtain. He checked on the passengers one last time, then slipped in to the galley. Rico hadn't noticed—yet.

"I thought I told you to get back to work."

"I am," she sputtered.

He shook his head. "Some people have to learn the hard way," he said, walking to where Jack sat.

What was he doing now?

Delaney saw Rico stop in front of Jack. She strained to hear their conversation. She couldn't make out the words, but the emotion behind them thickened the air until she could barely breathe.

Rico reached for his Glock, then pointed the barrel at Jack's head. Instead of recoiling, Jack stood to face him.

"Don't be a hero, Jack," she whispered, her heart threatening to explode.

Rico tapped and racked the gun, preparing to fire. *Nooo!* Delaney screamed silently as she reached under her pants leg to retrieve her pistol.

Everything seemed to move in slow motion.

Delaney raised her SIG Sauer to aim. She had a clear shot at Rico, but there was a good chance that if she took it, he'd still manage to fire a round and kill Jack. She whipped her gun between Rico and Jack. It seemed like an eternity, but was probably only a second or two.

Jack Gordon—expendable, echoed in her head.

Her orders were plain. Take out the main target no matter what. The situation was clear-cut in her mind. Delaney's world narrowed to black and white as it always had in her life. She aimed at Rico, placing his head in her gun's sight. She pictured Elaine's face and started to squeeze the trigger.

Too bad her heart had other ideas. Her clear-cut world switched to gray before her eyes. Delaney's hand jerked and she bumped the trolley with her hip. The cart wobbled and started to roll down the aisle, picking up speed as it went.

"Oh, God, no!" Delaney's eyes widened as she realized her cover was gone.

Everyone turned from the two men and focused on her. It was all the time Jack needed. He fought Rico, shoving him into the aisle in front of the oncoming beverage cart.

The steel contraption, which rattled like a hundred-and-forty-three-pound tin can stuck in a blender, bore down on him. Rico attempted to move out of the way, but wasn't fast enough.

It hit him in the thigh, flipping him like a pancake onto the top of the trolley. His weight didn't seem to slow its descent as it chugged like a runaway locomotive toward the back galley.

Delaney couldn't move. The cart traveled ten more feet,

then hit an armrest and abruptly stopped, sending Rico airborne. He sailed about three yards before landing with a loud thump into the aisle. His Glock flew over his head and out of his hand, spinning under a row of seats.

Delaney saw the curtain pull back slightly and Jeremy peek out. His eyes followed the weapon for a beat, then he moved faster than she'd ever seen him. He swan-dived into the empty row of seats, searching for the pistol.

Passengers craned their necks to get a glimpse of the action. Jeremy came up a moment later, gun in hand, then raised the weapon in triumph above his head. He grinned at Delaney, then started to hand the weapon back to Rico.

"No! Don't!" Delaney shouted.

Jeremy pulled back in confusion.

"He's the bad guy," she said, approaching at a run.

Jeremy smiled an evil grin right before he kicked David Rico in the chest with his Italian loafer. It was a testament to his anger that he hadn't stopped to consider that he might scuff the leather.

"Remind me never to piss you off, Jeremy," Delaney muttered under her breath, before asking, "Is everything okay back here?" She glanced at the closed curtain.

"Everything is under control," Jeremy said. His voice never wavered.

"Good. Can you handle this for a minute?"

"Sure."

Delaney handed him her gun with the frangible rounds and took the Glock. She didn't want Jeremy accidentally shooting himself. She headed back to check on Jack. She didn't think he'd been injured while fighting Rico, but she needed to see with her own eyes.

Jack met her halfway down the aisle.

Her heart swelled at the sight of him. "We have Rico," she said. Her fingers trembled as she touched his face.

He glanced over her shoulder. "I see that. Were you really going to shoot me?" he asked, his blue gaze boring into her.

"I didn't exactly have a choice." She rocked back on her heels and stared at him. "I couldn't allow Rico to kill you."

"So you were going to kill me instead?" he asked.

"My gun has frangible rounds in it."

He opened his mouth to speak, but she cut him off. "If you don't mind, can we talk about this later? I have to check on Barbie."

"Do you want me to do it?" he asked, compassion lighting his face.

She knew he was trying to save her from what might be behind the curtain. Delaney also knew that this was something that she had to do. "No, I'll go."

He nodded reluctantly, but the look in his eyes told her their conversation was far from over.

Delaney made her way down the aisle. Some of the passengers were crying, while others whispered questions, asking what was happening. Call buttons dinged throughout the cabin.

"It's over, folks. Everything is under control. We should be landing in Phoenix anytime now," she assured, not knowing whether it was true.

Her knees wobbled from the fear and adrenaline coursing through her veins. Delaney walked past the wayward beverage cart, which until now had been the bane of her existence, and patted the bent steel frame. She wondered if the airline would let her keep it when this case was over.

Jeremy hovered over David Rico in his best Dirty Harry stance, daring the man to move.

"Are you sure you're okay?" she asked as she neared him.

Jeremy nodded, but didn't take his eyes off Rico. "I've got him covered."

"Okay," she said, noting his steady hands. Newfound admiration filled her.

Jeremy flicked his gaze to hers for a second. "What?"

"What kind of shape is Barbie in?" Delaney asked, not really wanting to know the answer.

"Why don't you ask *Barbara* yourself?"

Delaney steeled her spine in preparation. She stepped over Rico, who still looked stunned, if his glassy eyes were any indication, then reached for the curtain covering the back galley.

She threw the curtain aside and gasped when she saw Tony sprawled out on the galley floor with airline issued handcuffs binding his meaty wrists. One of the metal coffeepots sat near his head, its base marked with blood. Barbie was on the jumpseat holding an emery board, filing away at her nails. Not a hair on her blond head was out of place and her makeup remained flawless, exactly like the woman in training had been.

Delaney gaped. She couldn't help it. She'd expected to come back here and see Barbara blooded and bruised, maybe even unconscious or worse. She'd expected to have to comfort a victim. That's what she'd braced herself for, trained for. Instead, Delaney saw a camera-ready woman, poised for her close-up.

"You want to tell me what happened here, Barbara?" she asked, finally finding her voice as the shock began to wear off.

She shrugged. "He reached below my Mason-Dixon line and tried to pick me up like a six-pack. You don't think you're the only one who attended the voluntary three-day self-defense training course for flight attendants, do ya?"

"I—I guess not," Delaney sputtered. She didn't even know there was such a class.

"Besides," Barbara said, flipping her blond hair over her shoulder, before leveling Delaney with a no-nonsense gaze, "that Yankee should've known better than to mess with Texas." She went right back to filing her nails without missing a beat.

15

JACK WAS WAITING when Delaney stepped out of the galley. "Is the flight attendant okay?" he asked, his gaze searching her face.

Delaney snickered. "She's better than okay." How could she have ever thought her crew was anything but competent? It shamed her to realize that she'd underestimated them both.

Delaney helped Jeremy secure David Rico with the only other set of handcuffs on the plane. They sat him up and strapped him into a seat, then wrapped the seat belt demo around his legs to keep him from moving.

That left one man to secure and Delaney had no idea how she'd do it. She made her way to the cockpit, shooting a glance at Jack as she walked by. He'd been comforting the passengers while she checked on Barbara. His gaze followed her, and she could feel the heat settling in the middle of her back, before dropping lower.

Delaney narrowed her eyes playfully. He didn't bother trying to hide the fact he'd been checking her out. She shook her head. How could he think about those kinds of things after what they'd just been through? Come to think of it, how could she?

Delaney smiled, then turned back to the task at hand. She needed to secure Rico's man in the cockpit.

She pressed the button next to the intercom a couple of

times and picked up the interphone. "Hey," she said cheerfully. "I wanted to check and see if you guys needed anything to drink before we land."

There was silence for a moment, then the phone crackled. "Yes, a couple of coffees would be nice. Bring them right up."

"You got it," Delaney replied. She entered the cockpit and handed a cup of coffee to the first officer, then pulled Rico's Glock. "ATF," she shouted. "Hand over your weapon."

Delaney saw the flash of surprise in the man's eyes, and then his gaze dropped to the coffee. "Don't even think about it," she said. Her finger stroked the trigger in warning. "Put down the coffee. It's over."

He hesitated.

"I'm not going to ask you again," Delaney growled out, fully aware that she'd kill him at this range and probably penetrate the fuselage.

"With your left hand, I want you to reach into your jacket and remove your pistol with two fingers."

The first officer complied.

"Captain, my name is Agent Delaney Carter. We have an emergency situation."

"What kind of an emergency are we dealing with here?"

"We have a cargo problem, sir," Delaney said cryptically, her mind going to the weapons in the belly of the plane.

"Understood," he said, then added. "Should I be worried about landing this bird?"

"I don't think so. We're dealing with criminals here, not psychotics. They wanted that cargo intact and they'd planned for us to land in Phoenix. I have to assume it's been stowed *properly*."

He nodded. "You don't sound sure."

"I'm not." The silence stretched between them.

"Roger that. Then we'd better prepare for an emergency landing."

Delaney's stomach clenched. She wasn't ready for this. She'd barely qualified with the FAA. The plane might not be full, but these people were still counting on her to save their lives.

"You better get a move on. We've been cleared to land," the captain said, before putting his oxygen mask on and answering the tower.

"Yes, sir." Delaney escorted the first officer out of the cockpit and left him with Jack, then made her way down the aisle to Barbara and Jeremy. "We have to prepare the cabin for an emergency landing. Hydraulics," she added hastily. They grabbed their emergency briefing cards, and then proceeded to reposition the passengers at the exits.

Delaney walked to the front of the cabin and turned the lights to full bright before picking up the mike. "Ladies and gentleman, the captain has indicated we're having mechanical problems and need to prepare the cabin for an emergency landing. I need you to place all loose items into the seatback pocket in front of you. Ladies, if you have on high heels, I need you to take them off and put them in there, too. Barbara and Jeremy are making their way through the cabin right now to ensure compliance. Please look at your emergency briefing cards to locate your nearest exit. Remember, it may be behind you."

Her voice quivered and her hands shook as she finished relaying evacuation instructions. If she wasn't trying so hard to put on a brave front, Delaney was convinced she'd have gone into the lavatory and thrown up.

Jack watched her with something akin to pride in his eyes. He hadn't said anything when Jeremy asked him to take his seat and buckle in, but she felt the strength that he silently lent her.

THE MOMENT THE WHEELS touched down in Phoenix, her week of training kicked in. "Heads down. Stay down. Heads down. Stay down. Heads down. Stay down," Jeremy and Delaney shouted in unison. They didn't stop until the captain came over the P.A.

"We're being taken to a position away from the terminal. When I give the command, I want you to evacuate the aircraft."

This was it. Everything came down to this one moment.

The aircraft stopped. "Evacuate," the captain said.

"Unfasten your seat belts. Unfasten your seat belts. Unfasten your seat belts."

Delaney was up and out of her jumpseat and assessing conditions outside the window. She swung the door wide until it locked against the fuselage, then grasped the safety handle. The slide inflated.

"Come this way. This way out. Leave everything. Come this way. This way out. Leave everything," she shouted as the passengers poured out of the exits.

The evacuation went smoothly. They got all the passengers off the plane in forty-five seconds. The only ones left onboard were Jack, Rico, Tony, the first officer and the crew.

Delaney looked down at the gathering agents with their guns drawn. She identified herself and tossed out all the weapons.

After the passengers were clear, Delaney detached the forward entry door slide so that stairs could be pushed forward. Agents rushed the plane, surging in like an angry swarm of bees. They swept for explosives in the cabin, while the deadly cargo was unloaded, then signaled the all-clear when it was safe for their superiors on the ground to board.

McMillan ambled up the stairs as the ATF took David Rico, the first officer and Tony into custody. Special-Agent-in-Charge Anderson waited on the ground, surveying the progress. The paramedics boarded next, giving Rico and Tony a quick check before being read their rights.

"Do you have a pair of cuffs I can borrow?" she asked McMillan.

"You plan to arrest someone?" McMillan asked, his gaze following Delaney's to where Jack sat.

"Temporarily."

"Sure you know what you're doing?" He glanced at Jack. "He looks like he's been through enough. The man hasn't taken his eyes off you since I climbed aboard."

Delaney took the cuffs from McMillan without answering, then strolled down the aisle. She wasn't sure exactly what she planned to do, but decided with her new way of looking at the world, that wasn't a bad thing.

Jack's eyes widened as she neared. "What are you doing?"

"What does it look like?" she asked, cuffing one of his wrists.

"You've got to be kidding? First you almost shoot me, now you're going to arrest me?" His expression held disbelief and staggering disappointment.

Delaney hardened her heart against the tug of emotions. She was doing this for his own good. "Tell me if this hurts." She clicked the cuff onto his other wrist, pulling his arms forward.

Jack cursed. "Yes, that hurts. I can't believe that you're going through with this." The accusation in his voice staked her heart. "What are the charges?"

She steadied herself and pulled Jack to his feet as David Rico and his goons were lead down the aisle. Rico grinned at Jack.

"I see I wasn't the only one fooled by her innocent face," he spat.

Jack scowled. "No, we were both duped," he said bitterly.

Delaney led Jack down the stairs and onto the tarmac. She stopped at McMillan's side. "Is there a car here that I can use?"

Away from the sedans with their flashing lights, he pointed

to a brown car off to the side. "You can put him in that one. I'll notify the agent that you're borrowing the car."

She nodded. "Thanks." Delaney took Jack over to the vehicle and propped him against the door while she reached inside to unlock the back.

Delaney opened the car door and stepped aside, waiting for Jack to slide in. His eyes smoldered with anger and betrayal as she shut the door behind him. Delaney prayed that after she explained, he'd forgive her. If not, well, at least she'd saved his life.

Now that Rico believed that Jack had been arrested, he could return home without fear of retaliation. Delaney watched as Barbara and Jeremy came down the stairs. She pushed away from the sedan and sprinted to meet them.

She stopped a few feet in front of them and grinned. They stared at her, then took in the melee. "You guys were terrific. I couldn't have done it without you," she said, stepping forward to hug them. "I'm sorry, Barbara."

"For what, darlin'?"

"For everything."

Jeremy was the first to pull back. "You want to tell us who you really are now, since it's painfully obvious you aren't one of us?"

"I thought I'd done okay."

He laughed. "Are you kidding? Barbara and I have been busting our humps to pick up the slack."

"Is that so?" Delaney asked.

Barbara looked at her and grinned. "Darlin', you leave a lot to be desired as a flight attendant."

"It's a good thing I'm an agent with the ATF then, isn't it?"

Jeremy's eyes bugged. "They let you carry a gun? Oh, my God, Barbara, catch me, I think I'm going to faint." He threw a hand to his forehead and wobbled dramatically.

The two women burst into giggles, connecting for the

second time that night. Respect shone in Barbara's eyes, reflecting exactly how Delaney felt. She'd been wrong about this woman, about flight attendants in general. They weren't a bunch of brainless trolley dollies with no skills. They were well-trained men and women who did a tough job and often weren't appreciated for it.

Delaney turned to Jeremy. "I thought you had a hot date waiting."

He straightened. "You know I do." He scanned the area. "Hey, isn't that the hottie from the plane?" he asked, pointing at Jack in the back of the sedan.

Delaney glanced over her shoulder. "Yes, it is."

Jeremy frowned. "I thought you two were tight or was that part of your cover?"

"Yes. No. I mean, it's complicated."

"It's going to get a lot more complicated if you're arresting him," he said, looking at her in confusion.

"I'm sure we'll work it out." At least Delaney hoped they would. She didn't know if Jack would forgive another betrayal, albeit temporary.

Fire lit Jeremy's eyes. "You don't have an extra pair of handcuffs, do you?"

"Jeremy!" Barbara nudged him with her elbow playfully. "I do believe you have a little kink in your tail."

He swiveled around. "Honey, you don't know the half of it." An agent approached and ushered them over to an awaiting van. "I guess that's our cue to leave," Jeremy said, eyeing the man's backside. "It was nice meeting you, Delaney Carson or whatever your name is."

Delaney shook her head and waved goodbye. She realized she'd actually miss them. Not enough to keep flying, but she would miss them.

McMillan approached, his ear buried in a cell phone. "Yes,

sir, that's right. We've apprehended the dealer and the contraband. Disaster averted." He glanced at Delaney. "Yes, we nabbed them, too. They were waiting on the ground, ready to unload the cargo, when we arrived. An L.A. unit retrieved the others twenty minutes ago. Thank you, sir." He snapped the phone shut and looked at her.

"Who was that?" she asked.

"Acting Special-Agent-in-Charge Griffin."

"Is everything is okay?" She wondered when Griffin had taken over the case.

"Perfect." McMillan grinned, a big beefy smile that turned his face into a pumpkin without the orange. "We about have it wrapped up here. The passengers and crew are being loaded into vans and taken for debriefing. We hope they won't speak to the media, but there's always one in the bunch who loves the camera."

Delaney nodded in agreement. "The only thing they can mention is the sky marshal incident. None of them know the truth about how close they came to dying. What about Special-Agent-in-Charge Anderson? He told me that I was to report to him on this case." She glanced over his shoulder at the scowling supervisor.

McMillan's expression grew fierce. "That was before he refused to send you the backup that you requested. He has other things besides Jack Gordon to worry about now."

"How did you know?"

He gave a sly smile. "I monitored the phone calls between you two, so that I could keep abreast of the case. I want you to know that you handled yourself like a pro during that evacuation," he said.

Delaney grinned. "Yeah, I did. Didn't I?" Newfound pride filled her. She'd conquered her fear long enough to do her job. With any luck, her fear of flying would be gone permanently.

"What do you have in mind for Jack Gordon?" he asked, curiosity in his brown eyes.

She shrugged. "Release him after Rico and the others are booked and transported."

McMillan cocked his head, his gaze piercing her calm facade. "I made sure they were led past the sedan holding Gordon just to ensure they got a good look at him. Rico laughed, convinced that Gordon was in worse shape. I'm sure he's going to try to lay the whole mess in Jack's lap."

"Let him try. We know better," Delaney said, defending Jack without thought.

McMillan's eyes narrowed in speculation. "He got to you. Didn't he?"

"I don't know what you mean."

McMillan watched her in silence until she started to squirm. "You ready to revise your earlier assessment of Jack Gordon?"

"No." Delaney felt the heat rise in her face. "I recruited him for the mission and that was all."

"Sure seemed like more to me. That wasn't anger flaring between you two on that videotape. I may be old, but I do recognize passion when I see it. You could always give a relationship a try and see what happens."

Delaney's hand trembled as she brushed her hair away from her face. "It's not like Jack and I have a snowball's chance in hell of making it. We're from two different worlds. Besides, Anderson would probably fire me."

"No, I don't think so. He couldn't legally do that. I reviewed the files on Jack. I even went back fifteen years. Like everyone else, I can't find an occasion where he actually broke the law. He certainly skirted it a time or two, but he didn't cross the line. And he wasn't behind the sale of the weapons that injured your sister. He was in another part of the world at the time, brokering a deal."

"I know. He told me," Delaney said.

He shoved a hand into his pocket. "So then what's been holding you back?"

Nothing. Delaney's heart leapt in her chest and began to pound hard. "What are you saying, sir?"

"Life's too short to live in the past, Delaney. Take it from a wise man who knows," he said reassuringly. "Don't use your sister's tragedy as an excuse for not living your life. I don't think your father ever intended for you to be unhappy. He wouldn't have asked me to look out for you, if he had. Your father is proud of you, even if he never tells you or shows it." McMillan pulled at his tie, loosening the knot as if this whole conversation was making him uncomfortable.

"Sir?"

"I'm saying that I don't see a reason for you and Jack to be apart. If that's what you want."

Delaney turned toward the sedan holding Jack. He was no longer looking out the window; he now sat staring straight ahead, a look of resolution on his face. She turned back to McMillan. "I'm not sure it'll matter what I want."

McMillan watched her, his brown eyes not missing a thing as emotions crested within her. "I can't believe a soon-to-be promoted GS8 agent would give up that easy. From what I can see, your mission is incomplete."

"Incomplete?"

McMillan handed Delaney keys to Jack's handcuffs. "You may need these later." He dropped them into her open palm. "I know you'll make the right decision," he said, before walking away without a backward glance.

It was the closest thing to receiving his blessing that Delaney could hope to get. She didn't really need McMillan's blessing in the matter, but it still made her feel better as she turned to stride across the tarmac to the awaiting brown sedan.

She climbed behind the wheel and started the engine. Jack didn't say a thing. He averted his eyes when she looked in the rearview mirror. Delaney pushed the hurt down as they sped off.

FOUR HOURS and several interviews later, Jack still couldn't believe that Delaney had arrested him. His shoulder hurt from being cuffed so long, but not nearly as much as his pride. He'd thought for sure that they had something good going, something more than just a case to put in a file to eventually be forgotten.

He'd been wrong.

Looking at her now only made things worse. She'd loaded him into another car to be taken to a different location. Jack hadn't bothered to ask her where. It no longer mattered.

This was the first time in his life that he'd misjudged someone. And it was the only time in his life that Jack had actually cared. That was the rub more than anything. Somewhere between Phoenix and Los Angeles, he'd fallen for Agent Delaney. Damn, he still didn't know her real name. How pathetic was that? Without volition, his eyes moved to the back of her head to stare at the soft glint of her hair.

She really was the perfect woman for a loner like him. Too bad she didn't know it—or care. He shifted, the cuffs biting into his wrists, sending pain through his nearly numb arms.

Jack replayed the moment in his mind. Rico had raised his pistol ready to fire right before Delaney hit the cart. He could still see her firing stance and the look of...terror in her eyes. He paused. It had been terror he'd seen, Jack was sure of it.

So maybe she cared a little.

Jack begrudgingly admitted that had she not shoved the cart, he might be dead. Rico wouldn't have missed at that close of range and he'd sure wouldn't have hesitated. Jack sat back, trying to get his legs to unfold in the close confines of the car. It was impossible to get comfortable.

He caught Delaney glimpsing in the mirror time and again, but she didn't say anything. What could really be said now that she was taking him to... He glanced out the window, trying to figure out where they were headed. One thing was for sure, it was away from downtown.

Was there a jail around here?

Jack didn't recognize any of the buildings as they wove their way through neighborhoods. He tried to spot the skyline, but it was impossible on the valley floor. He could make out a few mountains, but it was too dark to tell which ones.

They drove for what seemed like an hour, when it was probably closer to thirty minutes. Eventually, curiosity got the best of Jack and he had to ask. "Where are you taking me?"

She flicked her gaze to the mirror and seemed to debate whether to answer.

"Delaney, I know you can hear me. There are holes in this Plexiglas."

She pursed her lips, then took a deep breath. "I need to ask you a couple of questions before I answer you."

"Like what?"

"On my flights you were carrying luggage that you wouldn't allow me to stow. I want to know what was inside the bags."

"Are you serious?"

"Do I look like I'm kidding?"

Jack dropped his head forward in frustration. "I don't know what you want me to say."

"The truth would be nice," she said, turning a corner.

He looked at her. "I'm not sure which flight you're referring to, but the only thing in my carry-on luggage were clothes and a few pieces of art."

"Is that why you wouldn't let me stow it?"

Jack blew out a heavy breath. "I couldn't afford to let you stow the items. They were priceless."

Delaney nodded in understanding. "Now for the second question."

He shrugged. "Fire away, I'm not going anywhere."

"How mad are you?"

"What?" He had no idea what she was thinking with this line of questioning, but it was beginning to irritate him.

"You heard me," she said, glancing into her side mirror before changing lanes. "On a scale of one to ten, how mad are you?"

Jack looked out the window again, searching for a landmark he might recognize. "Eleven," he finally said. "Wouldn't you be, if our roles were reversed?"

She shook her head and disappointment flashed in her eyes. "You do know that I saved your life back on the plane. Right?"

Jack's jaw locked. As much as he hated to admit it, there was no sense in denying the truth. She had saved his life, even though her methods left much to be desired. "Yes, it crossed my mind," he said, reluctantly. "I also know that I saved yours. I'd say that makes us even."

She sighed.

"You want to tell me what's going on here, Delaney?" He inched forward as much as the seat belt would allow. "Where are you taking me? Why have you arrested me? I've gone along with everything that you've wanted. I answered everyone's questions. Signed all the reports. All without requesting counsel. What more do you want from me?"

Something flared in her eyes that he couldn't read, then she tilted her chin. "I arrested you for your own good."

"My own good. What kind of convoluted crap is that?" His voice rose along with his emotions. Jack didn't like being toyed with and she'd been doing nothing but toy with him since they'd met. "If this is some kind of game, you and the ATF will be in big trouble. My lawyers will have a field day suing you."

She looked away, but not before Jack caught the worry on her face.

"This is no game," she said, before adding in a whisper, "at least not to me."

That admission gave Jack a moment's pause. If this wasn't a game to Delaney, then what was she doing and where was she taking him? He looked into the darkened streets of Phoenix, attempting to catch the name on a street sign. Jack didn't know why he bothered since he wasn't very familiar with the city yet.

Delaney pulled in front of a small cinder-block house with desert landscaping. "This is it," she said, cutting the engine.

"This is what?" Jack asked, staring out the window.

"My home."

Realization dawned and the tense muscles in Jack's shoulders eased a fraction. He glanced at Delaney, then back at her house. "What do we do now?" he asked.

"I don't know. I'm in uncharted territory here."

"Are you going to invite me in?"

She turned to face him through the clear barrier. "I'm still thinking about it."

"What is there to think about?" he balked.

A small smile ghosted her lips. "Actually, we need to talk more first."

"I thought we'd covered everything, except the you kidnapping me part."

Delaney smirked. "I didn't take you for the dramatic type."

Jack snorted. "It's the truth and you know it."

She shrugged. "You're right. I did, but I had my reasons."

"And what were they exactly? I'm fuzzy about the details. Must be from the loss of circulation," he said, unable to keep a straight face.

"I almost shot you because I knew if I didn't, Rico would. He had the Glock leveled on your head."

Jack sobered. "I know. I was the one staring down the barrel. But that doesn't explain all this." He raised his cuffed hands for emphasis.

"That was for your benefit."

Jack blinked. He couldn't have heard her correctly. "Excuse me? Could you please repeat that last part?"

Delaney let out an exasperated huff. "It was for your benefit. I swear I've never met anyone as dense as you are, Jack."

"Well, then please explain for those of us too daft to understand."

She shook her head. "Do you want to hear this or not? I can drive you to your house and we can say our goodbyes there, if you'd prefer."

Jack's muscles tensed. As insane as this situation appeared, he wasn't ready to say goodbye to Delaney. Not yet. The thought had him straining against his constraints. "Continue," he said.

"I knew that if I allowed you to walk off that airplane that David Rico would have his men come after you. He'd know that you had sold him out. I couldn't chance him seeking retribution." She unbuckled her seat belt and began to pick at the frayed upholstery on the seat. "The easiest way to avoid that situation was to arrest you. Or at least appear to arrest you. That way Rico would think you were scammed, too. Why do you think my supervisor had Rico and his men led past this car?"

Jack took in every word. It hadn't occurred to him that they were putting on a show for Rico's benefit. Delaney had been looking out for him the whole time, which meant one thing—she cared. She might even *love* him. Jack grinned.

"If what you say is true, then why am I still cuffed?" he asked, dropping his voice to a husky tone.

Her pulse jumped in her neck. Jack followed the movement with his eyes, when what he really wanted to do was trace it with his tongue. He swallowed hard.

Delaney's gaze widened. "I needed to talk to you first and I didn't think that you'd listen if I let you go."

"Have some faith, Delaney."

"Like you had in me." The hurt poured out of her voice.

Jack took a deep breath. "I suppose we've both been quick to think the worst of each other."

She nodded. "Yes, we have."

"Do you want to tell me your last name now?" he asked.

"It's Carter."

"Well, Agent Carter, why don't you come back here and remove the cuffs? We can go inside and finish this conversation," he suggested, feeling his cock harden.

Delaney shook her head. "I don't think so."

Jack frowned. "Why the hell not?"

She smiled. "Because I haven't convinced you yet."

"Convinced me of what?"

"That I love you," she said in a hushed tone.

Jack stilled at her confession, his mind stirring with possibilities at all the ways she could go about convincing him. "You're right," he agreed. "I'm not convinced that you love me. You'll have to prove it." The statement threw down the gauntlet.

Delaney's mouth twisted in mock consideration. She tilted her head, sending brown hair cascading over her shoulder. "Convincing you might take me all night."

His gaze caressed her, taking in the curve of her neck and the gentle slope of her shoulders. Jack infused all the emotion he felt for her into that one look. Happiness filled him when he saw her breathing deepen in response.

He couldn't wait to strip the clothes off her body, feel her soft skin beneath his fingertips and hear her throaty cries of ecstasy ringing in his ears.

Jack licked his lips, looking forward to the night ahead and what lay beyond. One more night with Delaney would never do. Even one lifetime wouldn't be enough. All that mattered now was that she loved him. And he loved her.

Why else had he been willing to risk his life to save a stranger? He might not have recognized the emotion after their first night together, but his heart certainly had. And tonight he'd show her in a million different ways. He could hardly wait to get started.

Jack met Delaney's steady gaze. Her eyes twinkled in the low light. "All night, you say?" he asked, his body tensed in anticipation.

"All night," she repeated, a sexy lilt adding credence to her claim.

Jack nodded. "Promises, promises."

* * * * *

Enjoy a sneak preview of
MATCHMAKING WITH A MISSION
by B.J. Daniels,
part of the **WHITEHORSE, MONTANA** *miniseries.*
Available from Harlequin Intrigue
in April 2008.

Nate Dempsey has returned to Whitehorse to uncover the truth about his past...

Nate sensed someone watching the house and looked out in surprise to see a woman astride a paint horse just on the other side of the fence. He quickly stepped back from the filthy second-floor window, although he doubted she could have seen him. Only a little of the June sun pierced the dirty glass to glow on the dust-coated floor at his feet as he waited a few heartbeats before he looked out again.

The place was so isolated he hadn't expected to see another soul. Like the front yard, the dirt road was waist-high with weeds. When he'd broken the lock on the back door, he'd had to kick aside a pile of rotten leaves that had blown in from last fall.

As he sneaked a look, he saw that she was still there, staring at the house in a way that unnerved him. He shielded his eyes from the glare of the sun off the dirty window and studied her, taking in her head of long blond hair that feathered out in the breeze from under her Western straw hat.

She wore a tan canvas jacket, jeans and boots. But it was the way she sat astride the brown-and-white horse that nudged the memory.

He felt a chill as he realized he'd seen her before. In that very spot. She'd been just a kid then. A kid on a pretty paint horse. Not this one—the markings were different. Anyway, it couldn't have been the same horse, considering the last time he had seen her was more than twenty years ago. That horse would be dead by now.

His mind argued it probably wasn't even the same girl. But he knew better. It was the way she sat the horse, so at home in a saddle and secure in her world on the other side of that fence.

To the boy he'd been, she and her horse had represented freedom, a freedom he'd known he would never have—even after he escaped this house.

Nate saw her shift in the saddle, and for a moment he feared she planned to dismount and come toward the house. With Ellis Harper in his grave, there would be little to keep her away.

To his relief, she reined her horse around and rode back the way she'd come.

As he watched her ride away, he thought about the way she'd stared at the house—today and years ago. While the smartest thing she could do was to stay clear of this house, he had a feeling she'd be back.

Finding out her name should prove easy, since he figured she must live close by. As for her interest in Harper House... He would just have to make sure it didn't become a problem.

* * * * *

Be sure to look for
MATCHMAKING WITH A MISSION
and other suspenseful Harlequin Intrigue stories,
available in April
wherever books are sold.

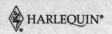

INTRIGUE

WHITEHORSE MONTANA

No matter how much Nate Dempsey's past haunted him, McKenna Bailey couldn't keep him off her mind. He'd returned to town to bury his troubled youth—but she wouldn't stop pursuing him until he was working on the ranch by her side.

Look for

MATCHMAKING WITH A MISSION

BY

B.J. DANIELS

Available in April wherever books are sold.

www.eHarlequin.com

nocturne™

The Bloodrunners
trilogy continues with book #2.

The hunt meant more to Jeremy Burns than dominance—it meant facing the woman he left behind. Once Jillian Murphy had belonged to Jeremy, but now she was the Spirit Walker to the Silvercrest wolves. It would take more than the rights of nature for Jeremy to renew his claim on her—and she would not go easily once he had.

LAST WOLF HUNTING

by RHYANNON BYRD

Available in April wherever books are sold.

Be sure to watch out for the last book, *Last Wolf Watching*, available in May.

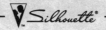

SPECIAL EDITION™

Introducing a brand-new miniseries

Men of Mercy Medical

Gabe Thorne moved to Las Vegas to open a new branch of his booming construction business—and escape from a recent tragedy. But when his teenage sister showed up pregnant on his doorstep, he really had his hands full. Luckily, in turning to Dr. Rebecca Hamilton for the medical care his sister needed, he found a cure for himself....

Starting with

THE MILLIONAIRE AND THE M.D.

by *TERESA SOUTHWICK,*

available in April wherever books are sold.

Visit Silhouette Books at www.eHarlequin.com SSE24894

REQUEST YOUR FREE BOOKS!

2 FREE NOVELS PLUS 2 FREE GIFTS!

Red-hot reads!

YES! Please send me 2 FREE Harlequin® Blaze™ novels and my 2 FREE gifts (gifts are worth about $10). After receiving them, if I don't wish to receive any more books, I can return the shipping statement marked "cancel". If I don't cancel, I will receive 6 brand-new novels every month and be billed just $4.24 per book in the U.S. or $4.71 per book in Canada, plus 25¢ shipping and handling per book and applicable taxes, if any*. That's a savings of 15% or more off the cover price! I understand that accepting the 2 free books and gifts places me under no obligation to buy anything. I can always return a shipment and cancel at any time. Even if I never buy another book, the two free books and gifts are mine to keep forever.

151 HDN ERVA 351 HDN ERUX

Name _____ (PLEASE PRINT) _____

Address _____ Apt. # _____

City _____ State/Prov. _____ Zip/Postal Code _____

Signature (if under 18, a parent or guardian must sign)

Mail to the **Harlequin Reader Service**:
IN U.S.A.: P.O. Box 1867, Buffalo, NY 14240-1867
IN CANADA: P.O. Box 609, Fort Erie, Ontario L2A 5X3

Not valid to current subscribers of Harlequin Blaze books.

Want to try two free books from another line?
Call 1-800-873-8635 or visit www.morefreebooks.com.

* Terms and prices subject to change without notice. N.Y. residents add applicable sales tax. Canadian residents will be charged applicable provincial taxes and GST. This offer is limited to one order per household. All orders subject to approval. Credit or debit balances in a customer's account(s) may be offset by any other outstanding balance owed by or to the customer. Please allow 4 to 6 weeks for delivery. Offer available while quantities last.

Your Privacy: Harlequin Books is committed to protecting your privacy. Our Privacy Policy is available online at www.eHarlequin.com or upon request from the Reader Service. From time to time we make our lists of customers available to reputable third parties who may have a product or service of interest to you. If you would prefer we not share your name and address, please check here. ☐

introduces...

Lust in Translation
A sexy new international miniseries.

Don't miss the first book...

FRENCH KISSING
by **Nancy Warren**

April 2008

N.Y. fashionista Kimi Renton knows sexy photographer Holden McGregor is a walking fashion disaster. And she's tried to make him over. But when they're lip-locked, it's ooh-la-la all the way!

LUST IN TRANSLATION
Because sex is the same
in any language!

www.eHarlequin.com

HB79393

COMING NEXT MONTH

#387 ONE FOR THE ROAD Crystal Green
Forbidden Fantasies
A cross-country trek. A reckless sexual encounter. Months ago, Lucy Christie wouldn't have considered either one a possibility. But now she is on the road, looking for thrills, adventure...sex. And the hot cowboy Lucy meets on the way seems just the man for the job....

#388 SEX, STRAIGHT UP Kathleen O'Reilly
Those Sexy O'Sullivans, Bk. 2
It's all on the line when Catherine Montefiore's family legacy is hit by a very public scandal. In private, she's hoping hot Irish hunk Daniel O'Sullivan can save the day. He's got all the necessary skills and, straight up or not, Catherine will have a long drink of Daniel any way she can get him....

#389 FRENCH KISSING Nancy Warren
Lust in Translation
New York fashionista Kimi Renton *knows* sexy photographer Holden McGregor is a walking fashion disaster. And she's tried to make him over. But when they're lip-locked it's *ooh la-la* all the way!

#390 DROP DEAD GORGEOUS Kimberly Raye
Love at First Bite, Bk. 2
Dillon Cash used to be the biggest geek in Skull Creek, Texas—until a vampire encounter changed him into a lean, mean sex machine. Now every woman in town wants a piece of the hunky cowboy. Every woman, that is, except his best friend, Meg Sweeney. But he'll convince her....

#391 NO STOPPING NOW Dawn Atkins
A gig as cameraperson on Doctor Nite's cable show is a coup for Jillian James and her documentary on bad-for-you bachelors. But behind the scenes, Brody Donegan is sexier than she expected. How can she get her footage if she can't keep out of his bed?

#392 PUTTING IT TO THE TEST Lori Borrill
Blush
Matt Jacobs is the man to beat—and Carly Abrams is determined to do what it takes to outsmart him on a matchmaking survey—even cheat. But Carly's problems don't *really* start until Matt—the star of her nighttime fantasies—wants to put her answers to the test!

www.eHarlequin.com